EL DORADO COUNTY LIBRARY

3  38  00411  3260

AR: 5.4    9.0 pts

D0014715

EL DORADO COUNTY FREE LIBRARY
345 FAIR LANE
PLACERVILLE, CALIFORNIA 95667

# Callie Shaw, Stable Boy

## A Novel

## by Judy Alter

EAKIN PRESS　　Austin, Texas
EL DORADO COUNTY FREE LIBRARY
345 FAIR LANE
PLACERVILLE, CALIFORNIA 95667

*For Fran Vick and Ellen Temple*
*with thanks for the Maggie Books*
*and, even more,*
*for friendship.*

FIRST EDITION

Copyright © 1996
By Judy Alter

Published in the United States of America
By Eakin Press
An Imprint of Sunbelt Media, Inc.
P.O. Drawer 90159  ★  Austin, TX 78709-0159

ALL RIGHTS RESERVED. No part of this book may be repro-
duced in any form without written permission from the pub-
lisher, except for brief passages included in a review appear-
ing in a newspaper or magazine.

ISBN 1-57168-092-6

**Library of Congress Cataloging-in-Publication Data**

Alter, Judy.
     Callie Shaw, stable boy : a novel / by Judy Alter.
          p.     cm.
     Summary: Callie follows her fierce determination to work with horses
by posing as a boy named Caleb and getting a job in a stable.
     ISBN 1-57168-092-6
     [1. Horses — Fiction. 2. Sex role — Fiction. 3. Texas — Fiction.] I.
Title.
PZ7.A4636Cal   1996
[Fic]--dc20
                                                                                    96-8490
                                                                                    CIP
                                                                                    AC

# Contents

# Chapter 1

# Dreaming of Horses

Aunt Edna said the devil would be amongst us when racing came to Texas, but I never believed her for a minute. In my mind's eye, I saw beautiful sleek horses thundering around a dirt track while people filled the grandstand to watch. Maybe some of the people had binoculars, which I thought would be pretty fancy, but they were mostly just plain folks like Aunt Edna and me, Texans out for a good time. I was unprepared for the splendor of Arlington Downs . . . and for the terror and joy it brought into my life.

Who would have thought that a little town in North Central Texas, suffering through the Depression of the 1930s, would have one of the fanciest racetracks in the whole country, with grandstands that seated 8,000 people and daily race purses of nearly $5,000?

Colonel W. T. Waggoner, a rich cattleman, built the track because he wanted a place to race Cowpuncher, the horse he declared was the fastest in the state. The story was that fire had destroyed his stables to the north, near Electra, and he moved the surviving horses to Arlington, where he established the Three-D Farm and then built the track and called it Arlington Downs. When the state legislature, desperate for income, legalized pari-mutuel racing in the spring of 1933, Colonel Waggoner had his racetrack ready. Presidents and princes came to the track and bet more money than I knew was in the world during that first three-week season.

But there were other people there, too, people like Aunt Edna who disapproved of racing and made their views loudly known. Others were as poor as we were, but not near as convinced about the devil — in fact, they seemed to think the Lord would smile on them at the racetrack. And there were people who made money whatever way they could and whose very appearance sent shudders of fright through me. I was, as it were, caught between them.

My name's Callie Shaw, short for Calpurnia. But nobody ever dares call me that, not even Aunt Edna, except when she's mad at me — and that happened more and more after Arlington Downs. My mother named me Calpurnia after a Scottish grandmother. My whole family came from Scotland. Aunt Edna told me that she and her husband and my father — her brother — and his bride came to Texas just before 1920, because they had no future in Scotland. They were so poor, they thought they'd starve. I always thought they were tenant farmers or something . . . until Aunt Edna told me the truth at last, but that's a part of my story later.

I didn't see that things were a lot better in Texas, but I never said that aloud. Sometimes I wondered, though, about the Highlands and my grandparents, who must have been left behind. No one ever said a word about them, and it left me feeling rudderless. I wanted a family tree that I could count on.

I lived with my aunt in a tiny frame house in Arlington, because my mother died when I was but a baby and Aunt Edna said my father asked her to take care of me until he pulled himself together. That was some thirteen years ago, and I guess he's still pulling someplace, but we never hear from him. Somewhere way back in a dim

2

memory, though, I remember my father and horses. All my remembered years I've had a fierce determination to have a horse. I've also had a fierce resentment of being poor, and the Depression hasn't helped it any.

Probably, when I broke that glass vase, my mind was seeing those sleek horses racing around the track, instead of seeing the knickknack shelf I was supposed to be dusting in the home of Mrs. Wiley Langdon. That's how she always introduced herself — never Emma Langdon but always Mrs. Wiley Langdon, as though it were a title, sort of like the Queen of England. Mr. Langdon, who had gone to his happy reward and left his sharp-tongued wife behind, was a rancher who must have had his money hidden in the barn because the Depression made not one dent in the way his widow lived. She had a cook and a maid — me — and a chauffeur to drive her Bentley automobile. Twice since I'd worked for her, Mrs. Langdon had been to Europe, each time bringing back nearly enough furniture to redecorate her entire house.

Every night when I went back to the tiny house Aunt Edna and I shared, my resentment of Mrs. Langdon grew. It wasn't envy, because I didn't want to be like her, and it wasn't self-pity, at least I didn't think it was. I didn't know myself what emotions rolled around inside my brain, but I surely did resent Mrs. Langdon and her knickknack collection.

When I turned fourteen, Aunt Edna had ruled that it was time I left school and went to work, since some nights we plain didn't have anything on the table but bread or potatoes and maybe some milk for me to drink. I was taller than usual, which made me appear older and therefore more likely to be a reliable employee. One of Aunt Edna's customers (she ironed clothes for a living) had told her that Mrs. Wiley Langdon was looking for a maid, and nothing would do but that I apply, nervously assuring the domineering lady that I was capable of dusting and cleaning. Aunt Edna forgot to tell her my age. I worked for Mrs. Langdon for six months, hating every minute of it, until I broke the vase. In the back of my mind, I knew I might have done that on purpose, just to get away from Mrs. Langdon, who insisted on calling me Calpurnia.

"It was just a piece of old carnival glass," I said defiantly, recounting the incident to Aunt Edna and omitting the fact that I could as easily have broken some of the fine English porcelain with which Mrs. Langdon decorated every available inch of tabletops and bookcases.

"That piece of carnival glass cost you your job, and Lord knows we needed that money," Aunt Edna said, her exasperation with me tinging her voice with anger. She sat on a straight chair before her ironing board, smoothing the wrinkles out of a heavy cotton boiled shirt as we talked.

"I didn't like working at Mrs. Langdon's anyway," I countered. "She thinks she's better than the rest of us, just because she's got more money."

"She's surely got that," Aunt Edna said dryly, "and I liked having a little of it to put food on the table for you. What now?"

"I'll find another job," I promised, though I swore I'd work for no more rich ladies, dust no more knickknacks.

"I don't know how," Aunt Edna said, her voice almost weary now, "with grown men taking any kind of work they can get and everyone leaving for California."

I looked at her and knew that she was worried and scared, and that she didn't mean to criticize me all the time, and that it wasn't her fault I went about with a chip on my shoulder. When I was little, she smiled a lot and sang to me. But these days she wore her fading red hair severely pulled back from her face, as though she was trying to will anything so silly as curls out of existence, and she always looked worried. Arthritis was creeping up on Aunt Edna fast, and she was beginning to stoop at the shoulders like an old woman, making her shorter than ever. Nowadays, she couldn't get around to do much

4

besides ironing, even if there were work available. I longed for her to laugh and sing with me again.

Back in the tiny lean-to that served as my bedroom, I lay on my bed and remembered that my father used to call me California. He'd laugh and say that was an Americanized version of Calpurnia, and then he'd swing me in the air and sing about Bonnie Prince Charlie in a rich, deep voice. Aunt Edna said I got my own voice, uncharacteristically deep for a girl, from my father. Maybe, I thought, California is where he'd gone.

I fell asleep dreaming of my father riding a sleek black horse and coming to get me. Always I'd thought of him as tall, with huge muscles that made him invincible. This time, in my dream, he was small and short, like a jockey. But he was richer than Mrs. Langdon, and he told me I'd never have to work again.

My uncle and Aunt Edna's husband, Charlie, died the year before Arlington Downs opened, and Aunt Edna blamed his death on the Depression. Oh, he wasn't one of those big executives who lost everything and jumped out of the window of a New York skyscraper. No, Uncle Charlie owned a feed store south of Arlington, where he'd worked hard for years and made friends with every farmer and rancher that came through the door. Only Uncle Charlie didn't really own the store — the bank did, and he made payments on a mortgage. When the Depression and great drought came, people had no money to buy the things they needed at Uncle Charlie's store, and he lost it to the bank because he couldn't make his payments. It broke his heart, literally. He died of a heart attack not a month later.

Like a lot of other people who were as hungry and poor as we were, I didn't understand about the Depression. I knew the stock market in New York crashed and all the banks went bust and all the rich men went broke. But that was New York and we were in Texas — and we weren't rich, that's for sure. We didn't have big banks and industries that closed. We had drought and dust storms that drove the farmers off the land and made everyone poor together. But the Depression was real clear in terms of Aunt Edna and me, because we lived from day to day, or, as she put it, "hand to mouth."

Aunt Edna worked from dawn to dark, doing other people's ironing and earning pennies for doing it. With some money she kept hidden under her sewing basket and what I earned from Mrs. Langdon, it was enough to let us get by. "We're fortunate some folks can still afford to send their ironing out," she said at least twice a day. It was her belief that people who formerly had maids and then lost money in the Depression washed their own clothes and sent them to her to be ironed.

But there was another side to the Depression — the Langdon side, as I began to call it. It was easy to call the Depression a great leveler of people since everybody had plenty of nothing, and they shared poverty together. But in Texas — probably elsewhere, but I didn't know about it — there were also wealthy people, who sailed through the 1930s untouched by poverty or hardship or want. I learned that lesson first from Mrs. Langdon and then from Arlington Downs.

"Hey! You can't go in there! There's a dollar gate fee!" The guard at the turnstile, motioning to me in a brusque gesture, was clearly angry. His look told me, in ways I could not fathom, that I was an outsider who didn't belong.

My purse held two dollars — money I'd kept back from Aunt Edna with a twinge of guilt for an emergency fund. I sure wasn't going to spend one of them on a gate fee. Thinking fast, I said, "My parents are back there," nodding my head behind me. It was a white lie, but it hid a greater lie. It was October 19, 1933, the first day of racing at Arlington Downs, and I had my heart set on seeing the horses run. I hadn't told Aunt Edna that I was going to Arlington Downs, drawn by my vision of those racing horses and my vivid dream of my father. In truth,

I'd let Aunt Edna believe that I was looking for work, maybe at the cafeteria where folks could still get a decent meal for under a dollar. My conscience was already bothering me, and the guard didn't help.

"Swell. You come back when they catch up with you, and I'll let you in. Till then, don't let me see you again. I can always call the cops." His voice made it plain that he did not for one minute believe my story about parents and that he wouldn't hesitate to carry through his threat if I tried to sneak in.

People pushed around me, laughing and talking, to pay their fees, enter the gate, and disappear into the crowd that thronged toward the racetracks. Suddenly, out of the noise of the crowd, one voice rose, shrill and high, warning, "Disaster waits for he who gambles. Turn aside now, repent and go home!" The speaker was a man who looked like all the schoolbook pictures of Abraham Lincoln I'd ever seen — tall and thin, bearded and rather gaunt looking. Even though the day was hot, he wore a full dark suit, crumpled and slightly stained. As he spoke he waved a handful of papers at people, most of whom simply walked around him without heeding his message. I wondered if Aunt Edna had been talking to him.

The attendant was even angrier about the man than he had been about me. "Hey! Get going!" He fixed his angry look on the man and began to shove him, while the man shouted, "Peace, brother, I come in peace to warn people against Sodom and Gomorrah!"

"Yeah, you warn 'em somewhere else," the guard said gruffly, pushing the frail man so hard he almost fell to the ground.

I wasted no pity on that strange man but used the diversion he caused to sneak through the gate and melt into the mass of people before the guard's attention returned to his duties. Somehow I found myself in the midst of a group moving toward the clubhouse. Trying to walk tall and look like I belonged, I stole glances at those around me and knew instantly that it was my cotton dress — washed and ironed until it was thin — that set

7

me apart. Most of these people were Mrs. Langdon's equals, which I should have known by the sea of fancy cars that surrounded the track. The women wore fashionable tunics and silly little hats, and the men had on shirts whose starch would have done Aunt Edna proud. Diamonds flashed in the sunlight, and binoculars hung around every neck — or so it seemed to me. The Depression wasn't real to these people, and they probably didn't know what the word "drought" meant, I thought bitterly.

I didn't know it then, but I was rubbing shoulders — literally — with Governor Ma Ferguson, the vice-president of the United States, who was a Texan named John Nance Garner, and the postmaster general. With a snort of disapproval, Aunt Edna read to me from the paper later that these politicians had been at the first day of racing. "Ought to be tending to the government," she said, "not running around supporting the devil's work."

From the top of the grandstand on the homestretch, I could look out forever, even see the pastures outside of town where cattle grazed and an occasional horseman rode among them. I spotted our house but looked quickly away because it made me think of Aunt Edna ironing and the fact that I shouldn't be at the racetrack. Anger flared again when I saw the Langdon house, a two-story white colonial with its driveway lined by arched trees. Closer to me, I stared at the track itself — a mile and a quarter, someone had told me, with an artifical lake in the infield. Beyond the backstretch was a second smaller grandstand, and to my right, a two-story brick clubhouse, substantial and solid-looking. My imagination filled in details of wood paneling, rich velvet drapes, and waiters in starched white coats who served champagne in fluted glasses. Mrs. Langdon was probably in there, drinking champagne and complaining about clumsy help.

Beyond the clubhouse lay the long buildings of the stables. From my perch, high as an eagle's nest, I could see activity bustling around the buildings: tiny stick figures walked graceful, prancing horses up and down in front of rows of stalls; other figures scurried in and out of stalls carrying buckets; jockeys carried saddles, stable boys combed horses (I didn't even know the word "curry" yet). It was a world I knew nothing of and longed instantly to join. That vision of my father riding a sleek horse floated before me again, and I knew with certainty that he was, somewhere, a jockey. It made sense to me that if I could attach myself to the stables at Arlington Downs, I'd eventually find my father, and then my world would be perfect, instead of the awful mess it was now.

Finally, I tore my eyes from the stable to look at the people near me. Here, in the stands, they looked less like Mrs. Langdon and more like . . . well, like Uncle Charlie. Cowboy hats dominated, worn by men in faded jeans and shirts. Oh, there was a sprinkling of women. Some in dresses near as faded as mine clutched the arms of their favorite cowboys. And there were a few people who dressed like they were pretending they were in the clubhouse. I was sitting next to a pair like that.

I was so busy staring at the people around me that I near missed the first race. It would hardly have mattered — without binoculars, the race was a blur, one horse indistinguishable from another. Around me, people jumped and shouted in joy or anger as they watched, but even if I had I a hundred dollars riding on a horse, I would not have been able to tell, from that distance, which horse it was. Maybe cowboys had better eyes, I thought, from counting cattle on the prairie. The man next to me, definitely not a cowboy, had binoculars. The announcer informed us that Altmark, a four-year-old chestnut gelding owned by Mrs. A. M. Creech, had won the six-furlong, $600 claiming event, in 1:13-3/5. It was Greek to me.

I stayed in the stands for the Arlington Inaugural Handicap, mostly because the announcer made it sound like such a big deal.

"What's a handicap?" I asked the man with the binoculars.

Startled, he turned to look at me, and then very earnestly tried to explain. "It's a race where you try to predict

9

who'll win by looking at the way the horses have run before . . . but it's really difficult, because these are only
two-year-olds. They haven't got that much of a record.
Still, the winner's share is over $1,400 . . . "

"Harvey!" A shrill voice rose above his. "Why are you
talking to that girl?" The woman dangled a cigarette
holder in front of Harvey, obviously waiting for him to
provide a light. Her hair was blonder than God intended,
and she had on lots of makeup. By contrast, I looked the
scullery maid that I had been until recently.

"Just explaining the handicap, darling," Harvey said
nervously and turned away.

"Thanks," I muttered to Harvey as I got up to leave,
but my thanks went unacknowledged and probably un-
heard. Darling had his attention.

As I threaded my way down the stands, I heard that
Bender First won the handicap in 1:12-2/5, paying
slightly over forty-six dollars on each two-dollar bet. Not
bad, I thought, wondering if I could make my living that
way — without Aunt Edna finding out, of course. The
things we think in jest often come back to haunt us, as I
found out later that afternoon.

Drawn almost beyond resisting, I drifted toward the
stables. In my mind I saw myself boldly talking to first
this jockey and then that, casually asking if they knew a
jockey named Bobby Shaw.

A large sign with red block letters proclaimed "Private: No Trespassing." Beyond that I could see a row of
stalls, each with a horse's head peering out through the
open top half of the dutch door. Wishing for a sack of
apples to offer, I was headed straight for the first stall
when loud voices stopped me.

"That's it, Benjie!"

"Show him!"

"The little bugger . . . !"

A chorus of shouts arose from behind the stables, and
I realized that I saw none of the bustling activity that I'd
noticed from the stands. There wasn't a soul in sight, but
the sounds led me straightaway behind the stables.

A fistfight was in progress. Two men — I couldn't tell their ages, indeed could barely tell which was which — were rolling in the dirt, pounding each other with their fists, pulling hair, and kicking in a manner that convinced me they were serious. Apparently every jockey and stable boy in the whole track stood around watching, cheering for Benjie, whoever that was.

Girls are raised to know that men fight — boys, we are told, will be boys. But I was surprised by the violence of this battle, the intent to do real bodily harm. I did what most girls would have done. I screamed.

The whole scene instantly froze, looking like a tableau in a wax museum. The onlookers turned in a mass to look at me, some literally with their mouths open. The two combatants rolled apart, stood on shaky legs, and stared. Then one of them shook his head as though to clear it, wiped his hair out of his eyes, and blotted at the blood on his lip. Slowly he came toward me, but there was no menace in him now.

"What're you doing here?" he asked warily.

"Looking," I said. "It was a fine show."

He looked just a little sheepish. "You're not allowed back here, 'less you're an owner . . . you're not, are you?"

"No," I replied, "just curious. I . . . I like the racehorses."

"You like the bangtails?" he said, smiling.

"Bangtails?"

"That's what we call them, the racehorses."

"Why?"

He shrugged as if to say he didn't know. "Just bangtails."

The others began to recover their voices now. "She's gotta get outa here," one said. "We'll all catch holy ned. Fightin's bad enough, but a girl in the stables . . . !" The idea apparently appalled him so that he was unable to finish his sentence, but his fellows seconded his opinion with a chorus of "Yeah." Then, almost magically, they disappeared, leaving the lone fighter standing before me.

"I'm Benjie," he said, twisting his hat in his hands. It

was a cowboy hat which he'd stooped to pick up. Now he tried unsuccessfully to reshape its bent crown.

"You're the one everyone was cheering for?"

"I guess."

I couldn't resist. "Who's the other one?" The "other one" had by now snuck away, limping as he went.

"Just another fellow. I reckon he's packing up his things now. He was . . . he wasn't takin' good care of Mr. Ferguson's horse."

Little did I know what those words hid, but I sensed that Benjie was honest and loyal. He was slightly taller than me and appeared to be slightly older but not a whole lot. He was too heavy to be a jockey, too poor to be an owner, neither handsome nor educated. Probably, I surmised, he worked here because he loved horses and because he could find no other job. And I doubted the "other one," who didn't take care of Mr. Ferguson's horse, would be back.

I asked him if he'd been working there long. "I been working over to the Three-D Farm for three years now," he told me. "Colonel Waggoner's kind of loaned me to Mr. Bertelli for the season. But when racing's over, I'll go back to the farm."

A thousand questions went through my mind — what did a stable boy do, how did you get the job, were girls ever hired? I was smart enough not to ask any of them.

"I gotta clean up," Benjie said. "Mr. Bertelli finds me looking like this, he'll sack me sure. You best go, Miss . . ."

"Callie," I said, "Callie Shaw."

"Right, Callie. Bet two dollars on Golly Gee," he said with a grin as he turned away. "He's a longshot."

I had no idea what a longshot was, but something compelled me to take the two lone dollars out of my purse, go to the betting window, and put my money on Golly Gee in the sixth race. Then I bit my nails and cursed myself for a fool through the next three races. When the sixth came, I was a nervous wreck and barely heard the announcer rattling off horses and owners.

Once again the horses were a blur, and I couldn't

12

pick out Golly Gee as they thundered round the track.
But I listened carefully to the announcer and nearly
whooped with joy when Golly Gee won. I made twenty-
three dollars on my two-dollar bet.

It was a fortune — and an embarrassment. What
and how would I tell Aunt Edna? It was one thing to hide
two dollars, but twenty-three? And yet, to confess that I
had gambled . . . With each step I took toward home, I
heard her bewailing the devil amongst us. Enough of her
lectures had sunk in to my consciousness that I knew it
was terribly dangerous to win, especially with your first
bet. It was liable to make you think you would always
win.

"I will never bet again," I vowed to myself.

The name "Ferguson" kept running through my
mind. Mr. Ferguson had lost his stable boy — or probably
so — and maybe he needed another. I knew nothing at all
about horses — only that dim memory from my earliest
childhood — but what could be hard about taking care of
a horse? By the time I got home, I had a plan.


"Aunt Edna, I found some work today. Here's fifteen
dollars."

"Fifteen dollars!" She was astounded and then suspicious. "What kind of work?"

"In the clubhouse at the racetrack," I said. There I
went again, telling a white lie. "There are real rich
people there, and they leave you tips. I . . . I only took
dirty dishes off the tables, but I worked all day." By the
time I'd walked the two miles from the track to home in
the late afternoon of an unusually warm October day, I
was hot and sweaty and tired enough to support that
statement. Would it, I wondered, ever rain again?

"Can you work there again?"

"Probably," I said, wishing she would just smile and
be happy about the money. "Here, I'll put this in the
sugar bowl for a special treat."

"Special treat? More likely we'll need it for food."
Then her voice softened, "But maybe we can buy a length
of cotton for a new dress for you."

I looked again at the thin cotton I wore and knew I
needed that dress. But right now my mind was on other
clothes. When Aunt Edna turned back to her ironing, I
headed for the shed behind the house where she'd stored
all Uncle Charlie's things and some of my father's. When
I opened the old trunk, the first thing I found was my
father's bagpipe — he had played it when I was small,
and the sound of a bagpipe could still reduce me to tears.
I held the plaid against my cheek for a long moment, and
then, putting it carefully aside, began to dig into the
lower layers of things. I pulled out shirts and jeans, even
a pair of workboots, and headed back to my room with
the treasures.

"Callie? Can you start supper?" she called from her
ironing board.

"Just a minute, Aunt Edna. I've been looking for
something in the shed."

Thank heavens Uncle Charlie had not been a big
man, no taller than my own five-foot-seven, and slightly
built. No doubt he had the perfect build for a jockey —
though Uncle Charlie had always been particular to
avoid horses. "I swore never to ride one again," I once
heard him tell someone. "I just sell supplies to them that
are fool enough to mess with the animals."

Wondering about jockeys and uncles and fathers, I
pulled on Uncle Charlie's worn jeans. They were baggy
but not beyond wearing, and I doubted that stable boys
set a standard of style. I took the clothes back to the shed,
folded and in a brown grocery sack, and left them near the
door. Then, singing a tune I remembered from my father,
"The Old Gray Mare," I headed for the house and supper.

"I swear," Aunt Edna said, "when you sing, you
sound just like your father."

"More like a man than a girl?" I asked.

"Your voice is pretty deep," she said without expression. I didn't know if she approved or not, or if my singing only made her long for better days, when Papa had sung.

I knew that I sometimes reminded Aunt Edna of my father in other ways — red hair, freckles, blue eyes that she used to say, with a catch in her voice, had the light of Scotland in them. But then she'd pull herself up straight as she could and say, "But those days are over, good riddance to him." I longed to ask her why he'd left, what made her bitter about him, why she would bid him good riddance when I waited almost breathless for him to return.

Instead, I asked, "What's for dinner?"

"There's some squash Mrs. Jacobs brought, in exchange for two shirts, and a pan of cornbread from the Williams'," she said.

I baked the squash with some brown sugar, heated the cornbread, and added beans left from the night before. That was supper.

"I'm goin' to the track again tomorrow, Aunt Edna, to see if I can find work again," I told her as we ate. It was all the truth, for once, though it was a slanted version.

"It's the devil's work," she said, "bringing that racetrack to Texas where we've got troubles enough without gambling."

"If it brings me work, surely it isn't the devil," I said, resisting the urge to add that those on the side of the saints hadn't done much for us lately. But when Aunt Edna sputtered unhappily, I was sorry I had spoken so rashly. That was my big trouble — one minute angry and bitter, the next guilty, one minute justifying a white lie to Aunt Edna, and the next agonizing over not telling the truth, as she'd raised me.

"Do you suppose," I asked, "that my father is a jockey?"

She looked long and hard at me. "Don't be goin' and gettin' romantic notions about that father of yours," she said too harshly. "He could be anything from a jockey to a con man, as charming and glib as he was, but you'll not hear from him again and more's the blessing."

I wished she hadn't said that. I wanted to believe that

15

my father would appear at Arlington Downs, a world-class jockey, ready to rescue me from the Depression. I didn't take into account the fact that by now my father would be getting a little old to be a jockey, and also that men were disappearing by the hundreds in these Depression days. Darn few of them were turning up to take care of abandoned daughters.

I went to sleep dreaming of sleek dark horses thundering around a mile-and-a-quarter track.

# Chapter 2

# Stable Boy Lessons

Reality was considerably different from my dreams. I rose even before Aunt Edna the next day, ate some left-over cornbread, and scribbled her a hasty note: "Back by supper. Love, Callie." I might have added, "I'm going to watch the devil walk amongst us and test him." Then, with a cotton dress pulled over my head and a sweater added against the cool morning chill, I headed for the shed.

At the shed I changed into Uncle Charlie's jeans, shirt, boots and added a cap that I'd uncovered among his things. The cap was big enough that if I pinned my hair first, I could hide it all underneath. I longed for a mirror but was afraid it would only confirm what I feared: I looked less like a boy than a girl dressed up as a boy.

As I hurried toward the racetrack, I tried to figure out why I was so all-fired determined to do exactly the thing that would make Aunt Edna the most unhappy. It didn't really, I reasoned, have to do with her. And it had less to do with getting a job than it did Mrs. Langdon — I wanted a job with what Aunt Edna would have called "prospects," though she'd have died a thousand deaths over these particular prospects. Still, if I could be around horses, and the people who owned them, I might recapture that remembered thrill from my childhood. And then, of course, there was my father and the thought that he might be a jockey. It was all too involved to figure out — I just knew that going to the stables that morning was something I had no choice about.

By 6:30 I was at the stables — no guard at the gate to stop me this time. Stable boys were moving about already with their morning chores, some getting ready to ride the horses out for exercise, others carrying feed and water. No one bothered me as I walked down one row of stalls and up another, but I had no idea how to find Mr. Ferguson. I had my answer ready if anyone had stopped me — a tough, defiant, "What's it to you?" kind of reply that I'd practiced several times, thinking it sounded right for a stable boy.

I longed to be past this first day, past the challenges and the questions and settled into taking care of a winning racehorse. I had no doubt that was how the day would end — and no doubt that whatever horse this Mr. Ferguson had was a winner.

Finally, I came across a stall with a small sign that said "Ferguson: Poco's Sweet Pride." Poco's Sweet Pride — that was his horse. I rolled the name around on my tongue, testing it and savoring it. And then I thought about the kind of person who would give a horse such a delicious name — no doubt he was tall, handsome, oh so sophisticated. Maybe he sang as he worked, like my father had, and maybe . . . maybe he had red hair like my father.

The top door was still closed to the stall that held Poco's Sweet Pride, so I couldn't even peek at the horse. Impatiently, I sat on a nearby bale of hay and waited. The man who finally opened the top half of that Dutch door was a distinct disappointment to me. I watched him approach — short and stocky, limping as though one leg were permanently shorter than the other, a cowboy hat perched too high on his head, his jeans and shirt rumpled as though he'd slept in them. He was probably, I guessed, about thirty — lots older than me, but not as old as Aunt Edna. But he whistled "Camptown Races" with a cheeriness that defied the early hour. And he sure didn't look like he belonged with Mrs. Langdon's crowd, which gave him a boost up in my books.

"Mr. Ferguson?" I pitched my voice as low as possible.

"Yep, that's me." He didn't even turn toward me but kind of talked over his shoulder.

"Hear you lost your stable boy yesterday."

Now he turned, surprised, and I could see a broad flat face, an incongruous background for eyes that seemed to be laughing, even in surprise. "That's right. So I did." He could have carried the conversation forward with a question about how I knew or what difference it made or whatever, but he simply waited. It was my turn.

"Looking for a new one?"

"You got any experience?"

I drew a long breath. "Never been a stable boy before," I said honestly, hoping that the implication was that I was familiar with horses.

"You like horses?"

I nodded, giving the gesture all the sincerity I could muster. Then, I added quickly, "My father's a jockey . . . in California."

He chewed on this idea for a minute. "How'd you happen to know about this?"

"I was around here yesterday when your former boy . . . uh . . . left," I said, thinking the less I said the better.

"Left?" He chuckled. "Way I hear it, Benjie beat him off. Lad didn't take care of the horse. I wouldn't have known if Benjie hadn't acted . . . and that's the kind of help I'd expect from you."

Even as I said "Yessir," I realized how inadequate I was for this job. What would I be expected to do? And what would Benjie do if I didn't do it?

"What's your name?" he asked.

Callie was on the tip of my tongue, so close in fact that I said "Cal" and only by fast thinking added, "eb."

19

And then, as though to correct my own mispronunciation, I said, "Caleb . . . Caleb Shaw."

"Well, Caleb, I'm Ker Ferguson. You can call me Ker."

"Cur?" I echoed. It sounded like a dog to me.

He grinned again. "Ker. K-E-R. It's an old Scottish name. My grandfather named me."

"Shaw's Scottish too," I said, warming to the man so that I nearly forgot my pose as a boy and was about to tell him about my full first name and how it embarrassed me. I stopped myself, mouth open, just in time.

"Sure is," he said enthusiastically. "We'll sing a song for the Highlands sometime. Meantime, let me tell you what goes on here. I own Poco's Sweet Pride, and I figure him to be a winner this season. Now, you and me, we can give this a try.

"Go fill this bucket with water at that faucet, and then come back and we'll feed. Then you can muck out the stall," he commanded, watching as I took the pail and turned away.

He stared at my hands, and belatedly I remembered Uncle Charlie's gloves which were in my pocket. Ferguson looked puzzled, but said nothing and turned back to his horse. So as I headed toward the faucet, I put my gloves on to hide the softness of hands that had done little besides dust knickknacks.

Benjie was ahead of me at the water. "Howdy," he said. "Name's Benjie. I work for Bertelli."

"Caleb," I muttered, "just going to work for Mr. Ferguson."

"No kidding?" he said with genuine pleasure. "He's a nice man, deserves a good boy. You do right by him, now!"

I nodded my head, filled my bucket, and went back to the stall, nervously aware that Benjie stood staring after me. I wished I could ask him what "muck out" meant, but I didn't think that would be smart.

If I'd told Aunt Edna what I was going to do, one of her cautions would have been that horses always recognize someone who's not used to being around them. I could hear her threaten, "They'll rear and kick, just to test you." I had no such problem. The very first minute I entered the stall, Pride — that's what Ker called him — and I were the best of friends. I stroked his nose, telling him how pleased I was to make his acquaintance and what good care I was going to take of him, and he nuzzled at my chest, pushing me ever so gently in what seemed like a sign of affection.

Ker showed me how to mash the oats with water to soften them. "Otherwise they'll go in one end and out the other without doing the horse much good," he said, grinning — and then he handed me a rake. Mucking out a stall became pretty obvious right quick. Pride stood perfectly still, watching me carefully with wide brown eyes that never missed a thing.

It was hard for me to relate this living, breathing horse standing in front of me to the kind of abstract animals that I had seen racing around the track the day before. And yet there he was, a horse in the flesh. Poco's Sweet Pride was a four-year-old, with a rippling skin of tan and brown so tight across his powerful muscles that it seemed painted on and a blaze of white on his nose to match his one white forefoot.

After I had fed him and mucked out the stall, Ker showed me how to curry Pride. The horse stood perfectly still while I brushed him, every once in a while turning to nuzzle me. This, I thought, is a snap. If this was all there was to taking care of a horse, I was in like Flynn. And I was finally around horses — to be specific, one wonderful horse. I thought I'd found heaven.

But it was far from heaven for the untried. By 10:00 in the morning, I was exhausted. I sank down against one wall, with Pride standing over me, and promptly drifted off into a dream in which I was riding Pride across a field — and being chased by Mrs. Langdon in her Bentley.

"Mr. Ferguson'll fire you, he finds you sleeping," a voice said, jerking me back to reality. Benjie stood before me, inside the stall. "You shouldn't let anyone else in the stall with your horse — 'specially not me, since I work for the competition."

"Well, then, get out," I snapped, angry at being caught and corrected.

He opened the lower half of the door as though to leave, paused and grinned. "Did you bet that two dollars like I told you to?"

My face flushed crimson, and I sank back down on the hay, almost speechless. "Will you tell?"

"Depends. Why're you here?"

"I need a job," I said truthfully. Well, at least, that was part of it.

"You ever ride a horse? No, let me put it this way — you ever saddle a horse?"

"No." My foot played nervously in the hay.

"Then why this job?"

"I . . . I like horses . . . and I lost my other job."

"Which was?"

Would he ever quit? I wondered. None of this was any of his business. Still, I answered, "Maid to a rich lady."

"So now you're stable boy to a rich man. Big difference."

There was a constant taunt in his voice that kept me edgy and uncertain. "He's not rich!" I countered. Somehow, to me, it would ruin everything if Ker was as rich as Mrs. Langdon.

"That's what you know about it," Benjie said disgustedly. "Poor men don't own racehorses. Come on, we'd better see that you can saddle a horse before you have to do it for your new boss."

For the next half hour, I had a lesson I couldn't have traded for, and at the end of it, grudgingly, I had some admiration for Benjie. He began by putting a hand on Pride's flank and moving it forward, always talking softly to the horse, praising him. By the time he put a saddle blanket on, Pride was nuzzling his chest, just as he had mine. And the horse stood still for the saddle, then the tightening of the cinch.

"Okay," Benjie said, "get on." His look told me plainly that he didn't think I could do it.

Determined to show him, no matter what, I put a hand on Pride's shoulder, talked gently to him, and raised one foot awkwardly into the stirrup. Pride whinnied and pulled away, dumping me in the straw. The horse pawed frantically at the ground, and I rolled quickly away from those sharp hooves.

Benjie laughed aloud. "At least you know to get out of the way. Try to the other side of the horse. Never mount from the horse's right."

A thousand retorts died quietly in my throat as I approached Pride again, talked to him gently, and put my left foot in the stirrup. By now, the horse was edgier than I was, and he pulled away again, still whinnying. This time I managed to keep my balance — but not my dignity — and stay upright.

"Okay," Benjie said, "you've never been on a horse. Right?"

"Wrong!" I said indignantly. "It's just been . . . a few years."

He eyed me skeptically, and I wanted right then and there to hate him. But I needed him too much for that. It struck me that I was being stubborn. I only needed Benjie if I persisted in this foolishness. If I just gave it up, went home and changed clothes, and looked for a suitable job, I could tell Mr. Benjie what I thought of him. Aunt Edna, I said silently, where are you when I need you?

"A few years," I repeated grimly. "Show me what I did wrong." It's hard to be humble to someone who makes you mad enough to spit.

"I'll hold the horse," he said patiently. "When you put your foot in the stirrup, do it with confidence. And swing quickly up, like you know what you are doing." He paused a minute, and then added, "Mr. Ferguson would have twenty kinds of fits if he knew I was using his pride and joy to teach a greenhorn."

"I'll learn fast," I promised grimly. And then I added, "He said to call him Ker."

"Fine enough for you," Benjie grumped. "He never told me that."

Learn fast is what I did, though the first time I tried to "swing up," as Benjie so casually suggested, I was appalled at the height of Pride's back. Still, on the third try, I made it, and Pride stood patiently with Benjie holding the reins.

"I got to get to work," Benjie said, abruptly walking away. "Bertelli'd fire me fast if he found me here. Good thing neither horse runs today. See ya." And he walked away, leaving me seated on Pride. Benjie's quick backward glance convinced me he knew exactly what he was doing.

Heart pounding but voice as quiet as possible, I got my feet back onto firm ground, got the saddle off and back on the pegs, and collapsed in a heap in the straw. Pride nuzzled me as though to ask what the matter was.

It's that darn Benjie, I wanted to shout.

When Ker came round to check, he found me polishing the saddle, something I'd figured out all by myself when I found the saddle soap. "Good, good," he said happily, so pleased that he added, "You handle the horse real well. Guess you better plan on riding out to exercises in the morning."

My heart sank. I could probably get on Pride, but how would I steer him?

There was nothing I wanted to do less than find Benjie and ask his help, but the more I considered my choices, the narrower they got. I couldn't confess to Ker that I'd never, within my real memory, ridden a horse. Oh, I could have just walked away and forgotten the whole thing — food on the table probably didn't depend on my riding a horse, Depression or no. And in fact walking away would have at least put me in Aunt Edna's good graces, if I ever got the nerve to tell her the whole story. But something strong inside me was determined to see this through — for lots of reasons, finding my father not the least among them.

"See you in the morning, Caleb. I'll be real interested to see how you do in exercises," Ker said, and though I wanted to glower at him, I knew he meant it the right way. He wasn't testing me or trying to trip me. He really wanted to know what kind of stable boy he'd hired. And he had a right to know.

"Hey, Benjie!" I put all the bravado I could muster into calling out to him in as low a voice as I could manage. At the end of the day, the stable boys all apparently congregated outside the stalls, maybe to hash over the day, maybe to complain about their trainers, who knows what? I only knew I wasn't part of it, and there I was trying to call Benjie away.

"Come on and set a spell," Benjie said, though I thought his eyes had a gleam in them, as though he wanted to see how much I'd mingle with the other boys.

"Sure," I said casually and managed to shake hands — with my gloves on — and nod my head as I was introduced to them. There was T. Joe, dressed in cowboy clothes and full of swagger, and Lonnie, the smallest of the lot though maybe the sharpest with a tongue to match his brain, and Walter, large and not too bright, and then a couple of others whose names went by me. I sat, and we chatted about the horses — who was winning, who was losing, how the bets were going. I was amazed at how much the stable boys knew about the whole track.

The group sat for another fifteen minutes or more, and I got to refuse a cigarette — "What's the matter, you don't smoke?" T. Joe asked indignantly, and muttered something unprintable when I confessed that no, I didn't smoke. "Ought to try it," he said. But I noticed Benjie wasn't smoking either, and that maybe made it all right.

Finally, they began to drift one way and the other, and I managed to pull Benjie aside. Before I could say anything, he grinned at me and said, "You're doing right well, uh, Caleb."

"Thanks. But Ker wants me to ride in the morning."

25

"Uh-oh," he said, "Armegeddon. What're you gonna do?"

I squelched the urge to kick him. What in heaven's name did he think I was going to do? "Ask you for help," I said.

He looked a little nervous. "I . . . well, there's this girl . . . she's waiting for me . . ."

"Five minutes," I said disgustedly, "just a five-minute lesson. She'll wait."

He ended up spending an hour. First, he made me saddle and mount Pride, amidst groans of "If Mr. Ferguson finds us, we'll both be on the dole," and "I can't believe I'm doing this." Then it was strictly business. "Cluck to him, softly . . . tell him he's good, how proud you are of him."

Pride began to move out of the stall, and I had to bite my tongue to silence a yelp of joy. Within minutes, I learned to guide him by the reins, walking him this way and that. Then Benjie talked about using my knees to signal different gaits. I wasn't exactly a success, but we did manage a fast walk around the stables.

"Maybe," he said dispiritedly, "he'll see the other horses running out in the morning and follow them. I can't see you pushing him into a gallop."

"I love it!" I cried. "I'm a natural . . . I was meant to be on the back of a beautiful horse."

Benjie shook his head. "Hold on, now, Callie . . . er, Caleb. You done right well for a beginner, but you still got a lot to learn . . . a whole heck of a lot."

"What?" I demanded with the belligerence that comes of a little knowledge.

"A lot about the feel and moods of a horse," he said, "and there ain't no way I can teach you that in five minutes. Besides, my five minutes is up."

"You're riding that horse without permission! I'm gonna tell!" The threatening shout came from behind us, startling Pride so that he shied and I nearly lost my seat, hanging on only by grabbing his mane . . . and praying aloud.

"Hah! I knew she'd fall!" T. Joe came swaggering up to stand within inches of Benjie's nose, while I, having heard the word *she,* froze in the saddle.

Benjie looked calmly at T. Joe, and because he had an inch or two on him in height, he was able to look down with great psychological advantage. "You'll tell what?" he demanded calmly.

"Well," T. Joe said, hooking his thumbs into his pockets in a manly gesture, "that the new stable boy is a girl for starters . . ."

"And how," Benjie asked, "do you know that?"

"Ah, I can just tell. Look at her . . . too frail to be a feller."

I opened my mouth in protest, but a look from Benjie silenced me. "Well, I guess you're the expert," Benjie said slowly, "but how about if that so-called girl offers to fight you fair?"

T. Joe jumped a little. "Fight me?"

"Yeah, just like I fought Willie yesterday." Benjie looked at me, "You willing, *Caleb?*"

Once again I really concentrated on pitching my voice low. "Sure," I said, rubbing one open palm over a closed fist in a gesture I thought bespoke defiance.

T. Joe, for all his swagger, was a coward. "Ain't no need to fight," he said nervously. "I didn't mean nothin'. . ."

"You ever call Caleb a girl again out loud, and you'll fight him," Benjie said threateningly.

T. Joe was almost but not quite ready to quit. "Mr. Ferguson'd have fits he knew she . . . uh, he . . . was riding late like this."

"Have you discussed this with Mr. Ferguson?"

"Well, uh, no . . . I just know . . ."

"T. Joe, you don't know a thing," Benjie said, "and you best get out of my sight *now!*"

T. Joe left . . . and I laughed so hard I got careless with my seat and fell off Pride. It scared Pride so that he reared and might have struck me without meaning to if Benjie hadn't yelled, "Roll, Callie, roll!" I obeyed without thinking and was clear of the hooves when they came

27

down. Benjie grabbed the reins and began to calm the frightened horse, while I sat up, shivering at the close call I'd had.

"You okay?" Benjie asked.

"Sure," I lied, determined not to let him know how scared I was. Belatedly, I remembered that in that instant of fright, Benjie had called me "Callie," not "Caleb." He never would learn to think of me as Caleb, and I wasn't sure if that was good or bad. For one thing, he probably wouldn't help Caleb as much as he would Callie, and I intended to take advantage of that.

To my relief, he said, "Lesson's over for today. You'll be all right in the morning." Turning to lead Pride back to the stall, he said, "Come on, come on, I haven't got all night. We got to get him curried and calmed down."

Once in the stall, he never said a word, just picked up a brush and began working on the horse, while I, still shaking, sat in a corner of the stall. Finally, I could manage a weak, "Why are you doing this for me?"

"Not for you," he said shortly. "For Mr. Ferguson. He's one of the best men I ever met."

"Oh." My reply was faint, without understanding.

"You don't understand about him," Benjie said. And he launched into the story of Ker Ferguson, would-be racing tycoon who was, in reality, a rancher's son, from a family who thought that horses were used only for herding cattle and that racing, especially pari-mutuel betting, was sinful. They disapproved of everything and most particularly of Ker's determination to race. As Benjie talked, I pictured a grim-looking couple, sort of like that famous Grant Wood painting, *American Gothic,* we'd studied when I was still in school.

"The Depression?" I asked. "Are they hurting for money?"

He gave me a pitying look. "Not on your life. They got more money than Midas has gold, but they sure don't give it to Mr. Ferguson. He's got to earn every inch of his way. They just got this silly notion that anything they don't understand is evil."

28

"My aunt says the devil walks amongst us now that racing has come to North Texas," I said suddenly.

He looked startled. "Does she really believe that?"

"I think so," I said, rising from the straw. "Here, let me do that. You're already late for that girl."

"What? Oh, yeah, I better be going," he said, suddenly seeming a little flustered. "I'll . . . I'll see you in the morning."

"Yeah," I said, "and Benjie, thanks." I wasn't much at putting thanks into words, but in a world where I'd come to expect that nobody did anything for anybody else without selfish motives, Benjie was a surprise.

Suddenly, something dawned on me. As he left, I called out, "What's your last name?"

"Thompson," he called back.

Another Scot, I thought. Was Texas that full of us?

I stayed in the stall, currying Pride and talking to him, for almost another half hour. I would probably have stayed longer if T. Joe hadn't walked in, unannounced and uninvited. Benjie's absence apparently made him bolder.

"You'll be sorry," he threatened. "When something bad happens to this horse, you're going to get the blame."

My anger flared, and I grabbed the nearest weapon — the pitchfork — brandishing it in his direction. T. Joe fled without a word, and only after he was gone did I realize he'd said "when," not "if." Did he know something? Was something bad going to happen to Pride?

# Chapter 3

# Poco's Sweet Pride

It had been an extraordinarily long day. The two miles to home seemed longer than ever, and by the time I dragged myself into the shed, I had been gone from home over fourteen hours, and I was exhausted. Carefully I folded Uncle Charlie's clothes and slipped back into my dress, thanking the stars that Aunt Edna wasn't limber enough to come searching for something in the shed. Then, sneaking around the side of the house, I entered the front door, the weary worker returning from her labors.

Aunt Edna sat in the dark, no lamp lit, though dusk had come.

"Aunt Edna? You all right?"

"I suppose," she said, her tight lips betraying her words. "I . . . I was worried about you. Waitresses don't usually work such long hours."

"Racetrack is different, Aunt Edna. They let us work long shifts, maybe 'cause we can only work there three weeks." I lied easily. No need to wonder what she'd say if she knew the truth.

"You get paid as well today?" she asked suspiciously.

I hadn't thought of that. Having once given her

money, she'd expect it every day. "No. Boss said he'll pay once a week from now on. But I bet I earned real good money today." I hadn't even asked Ker what the pay was or when I'd be paid. Some businessperson I was!

"I hope," she said and sighed. "The Vandermans quit me today. She says she can't afford to send ironing out anymore, goin' to do her own."

"Mr. Vanderman will look a rumpled mess," I predicted with a slight laugh. He was a portly man with huge shirts that had to be starched stiff as boards because he literally wore them into wringing wet messes, even in cold weather.

"That's not funny," Aunt Edna said sharply. "I did ten shirts a week for him . . . that's a lot of my income."

It struck me that I was always amused at the wrong time . . . or maybe it was that Aunt Edna was never amused anymore. If the Depression went away tomorrow, I wondered, would Aunt Edna go back to singing songs?

I went to where she sat and put an arm around her shoulders. "I'm sorry. I know it's not funny, and I know you're worried. It'll be all right. I'll bring home more money than you need." An exaggeration, but . . . .

I longed for a pat on the arm, a smile, a thank you because she knew I was working hard. Instead Aunt Edna simply sat still and said, in her strained voice, "Would you see to supper?"

To cheer myself, I sang "Scotland the Brave" — a song my mother had taught me when I was still nearly in the cradle, because my father played it on the bagpipe. It always brought me visions of strong men, wearing kilts, marching across the Highlands, and I was comforted to think I was descended from such. More than that, it made me feel close to my parents, however briefly. Now it made me think of Ker Ferguson and Benjie Thompson, almost as though they were part of that family tree I longed for. Still, I wished Aunt Edna would say more than simply good riddance to my father.

"Please, Callie, I have a headache already," Aunt Edna said, and I stopped singing.

31

I must remember, I thought, not to sing in the stables, for I sound very much like a girl when I sing.

We had fresh green beans, from a neighbor's garden, and biscuits for dinner, served with watered-down tea. Aunt Edna hoarded tea and reused it until the pale brew tasted of nothing but water. But it comforted her to drink tea, or what passed for it.

I went to bed with my thoughts tumbling — Benjie and T. Joe, Ker Ferguson, Aunt Edna and her determined unhappiness — and I fell asleep before I could think about any of those things. I slept so soundly that the sun was well up when I woke. I bolted out the door with a hurried farewell called over my shoulder, managed a record-time change of clothes in the shed, and ran as much of the way to the stables as I could, slowing too often to catch my breath. Dusting knickknacks had not exactly put me in shape for vigorous exercise.

Without seeing them, I ran past small houses like ours, on unpaved streets, past the tiny strip of stores that was the so-called business district in Arlington, and onto the open road that led to Arlington Downs. On my right as I ran was Colonel Waggoner's Three-D Farm. Several horses grazed in the pasture, oblivious of my frantic haste.

Ker was waiting, looking at his watch, peering toward the gate from time to time, and looking generally impatient.

"He's going to sack me," I thought as I paused to catch my breath before approaching him.

"Caleb," he said heartily, "I was worried about you. Thought yesterday had been too much, and you'd changed your mind."

"Overslept," I mumbled. "Sorry. It won't happen again."

Those laughing blue eyes looked at me. "You ready to ride?"

"Uh, sir, wouldn't you rather exercise Pride yourself?" It was a desperate hope, one I'd dreamed up as I ran toward the stables that morning.

"Nonsense. Want to see what you can do." He hooked his thumbs into his jean pockets and nodded. "I'll see you at the track." With that he limped off, whistling "Danny Boy."

Morning exercises were a disaster. My sense of self-confidence and my feeling of being at home on a horse's back, so new to me just yesterday, had vanished. I was uncertain, half afraid of falling off, utterly without common sense. Pride ran without guidance because I had no idea how to direct him. He veered into another horse, earning me a sharp curse from T. Joe and a look which clearly threatened to reveal my secret.

Since exercises were conducted at a civilized pace — almost leisurely compared to racing — stable boys could talk to one another as they passed or rode. Benjie rode near me twice, with muttered commands like, "Firm hand on the reins" or "Sit up straight, look like you're in control." I tried, harder than anyone knew, because I was embarrassed to be a failure — and because I very much wanted this job.

I did have a chance to see the *other* boys — that phrase went through my mind and tickled me so I nearly laughed aloud. T. Joe rode a chestnut with three white stockings. To my untrained eye, the horse was only a fair horse, lacking somehow the sense of pride that my mount had. Pride seemed to live up to his name. And T. Joe rode awkwardly, not like Benjie, who seemed to become one with the dark bay he rode, riding so comfortably that what was not casual looked that way. He didn't slouch, and he didn't look bored. There was a sense of control about his riding that I admired mightily.

Something spooked Pride. A mouse in the grass? A bird in the trees? Whatever caused it, Pride took off suddenly, as though the devil, instead of walking amongst us, was right on his tail.

I grabbed the reins, and instinct made me hunch down behind his neck. Then all I could do was hold on. Almost frantic, the horse circled the exercise track twice.

What was probably just minutes seemed hours as I

clung to Pride's neck, the wind whipping my hat until I had to let go of the reins with one hand and hold the hat. If the hat blew off my long hair would be uncovered. All my resolve to whisper sweet nothings in Pride's ear were forgotten in my desperation, and I shouted frantically for him to stop. Visions of terror flew through my mind: Pride leaping a fence and taking off across the adjacent pastures, Pride stumbling in his breakneck pace and falling on top of me . . . or worse yet, breaking a leg. Between shouting at the desperate horse, I said a few quick prayers.

They must have been answered. As suddenly as he'd started, Pride stopped and stood with sides heaving, sweat running.

Ker arrived on a run, a funny gait for a man of his shape. "Caleb!" It was the sharpest tone he'd used with me yet. "You can't handle a blowout run."

Having barely recovered my breath, I stared down at him from my high seat. "Ker, I didn't run him. He ran me." I had no idea that a blowout was a real fast short run for a horse that was about to race. To me, the whole thing had been an accidental disaster.

"Walk him back to the stall and rub him down good," was his only reply.

I dismounted — well, almost slid off the horse — and led him away, my knees shaking badly but my presence of mind recovered enough that I could talk softly to calm him. Pride must have understood my words, for though I talked calmly I told him, in plain language, that he was a darnfool horse that nearly broke my neck and if he ever did anything like that again I'd see that he was sent to the packing plant. He was jittery and jumpy, shying sideways and making me hold tight to the rein I held. Sometimes he'd snort a little, as if in indignation, and once he whinnied loudly as though calling for help.

I looked straight into his eye and saw that he was terrified — of me! "Oh, Pride," I said, sighing, "I didn't mean that. I know you didn't mean to scare me. Something scared you. You're gorgeous, and I'll never let anyone hurt you . . . let alone send you to the packing plant!"

He calmed down almost immediately, and the eerie realization came to me that Pride really did understand what I said. I'd never tell Benjie that — he'd laugh me out of the stables.

Ker followed us, fortunately not close enough to make out what I first said to Pride. Then a dark-haired, dark-skinned man wearing slacks and a jacket stopped him — grabbed his arm, really — and began to gesture wildly at him. I didn't know why the man's appearance both fascinated and scared me, except that he didn't look like a Texan — no hat, no boots, no jeans. I was just far enough away that I couldn't make out the conversation, only an occasional word, such as "danger" and "responsibility." The man was obviously angry almost beyond bearing, but Ker simply stood and looked at him, nodding occasionally, and apparently answering with a murmur.

I put Pride in his stall, gave him just a bit of water, and began to curry him, though he was still nervous. My conversation with him now dwelt on what Ker would say when he returned to the stall.

What he did say surprised me so much I dropped the brush. "Bertelli," he said, "demanded I give you the sack immediately. Says you're a danger to the other boys and to the horses. Got anything to say?"

"No," I muttered. Way back in my memory, I recalled Aunt Edna saying a teaspoon of sugar caught more flies than a cup of vinegar. I should, I knew, have turned toward Ker, with some well thought-out explanation . . . or at least something to say. Instead I kept on brushing. Stubborn, Aunt Edna would have said.

"Should I sack you?" he asked, coming around Pride so that he could look me in the face. He was neither smiling nor angry. Instead, he looked like he needed my opinion.

"It's up to you," I said. I wanted to be angry — at Pride, Bertelli, even Ker Ferguson, who didn't deserve it and should, by rights, have been seething with anger at me instead of calmly asking my opinion about whether or not I should be fired. Instead, Ker Ferguson's look made me humble. That was an unaccustomed feeling for me. "I made a botch of it, and I admit that." The words came out in a short, unapologetic tone.

Bless him, Pride chose that moment to calm down and push his nose against my chest, a sign of support for me.

"You haven't ridden a lot, have you?" Ker asked.

"No," I said, "I haven't."

"But you let me believe you had."

"I guess so."

"Why?"

"I wanted to work in the stables . . . I like horses." I faltered.

"Pride is pretty valuable to take a risk on with a tenderfoot," he said, still without the anger that was by rights his, "but I'll trust you . . . and obviously Pride already does."

"I . . . I'll see that he's well taken care of."

Only then did Ker's mouth tighten, losing its characteristic smile. "Bertelli doesn't tell me what to do," he said, after a pause. "Tell me how the horse got away from you."

"I have no idea," I answered honestly. "One minute we were going along — not very well, I admit — and the next he was racing."

"And you're too green to stop him." He seemed to ponder that for a long minute.

Suddenly, honesty seemed important to me. "Ker, I did lie to you, but if Pride loses the race today because of me . . . well, the least I can do is promise that you'll never see me again. And," I added bravely, "you don't have to pay me for the two days."

"Thanks," he said wryly. "Let's just not tell Chance about this morning's incident."

"Chance?" I asked blankly.

"He's the jockey who'll be riding this afternoon. No need to alarm him. Pride looks fine now. I . . . well, I'm going up to the clubhouse. See how the betting's goin', if nothin' else."

Pride stood quietly, and I sank into the hay, relieved

that I had not lost my job. I felt overwhelmed by the responsibility of Pride.

"You alive?" Benjie stuck his head around the door.

"Yeah," I said, "I am."

"Get the sack?"

"No."

He shook his head. "Bertelli would've sacked me so fast I couldn't have seen the difference between daylight and dark." He sank down on the hay beside me.

"Bertelli told Ker to sack me, practically ordered him," I said, picking idly at a bit of hay on my pants leg.

That interested Benjie. "No kidding? Well, I'll be . . ." But his voice trailed off and I never knew what he thought was important about that. He studied on it for a long minute and then said, "Could one of the other boys have spooked him somehow?"

I stared at him, open-mouthed. "Why would they do that?"

"It's a possibility. I heard T. Joe talking too loud about how you're a girl and shouldn't be here. Maybe he thought he'd frighten you away."

"Well, it won't work," I said, anger rising. "Ker said he trusted me . . . and I won't let T. Joe or anyone frighten me away."

Pride bent his nose down to the top of my head, as though to display his trust in me.

"Pride runs today and Golly Gee doesn't," Benjie said. "I'll watch the race with you."

"You mean," I asked, "that the horse you told me to bet on is the one you look after?"

"You just now figuring that out?" he asked.

Benjie was a little bossy in announcing we'd watch the race, but still, I was pleased at his semi-invitation. "Are you going to tell me to bet again?" I asked, my spirits returning just a bit.

"Two dollars," he said, "no more. On Poco's Sweet Pride."

"Is he a . . ." I stumbled over the word. "A longshot?"

"Yeah," Benjie said, "he is."

37

Pride stood tall and straight, his head up, and I knew he would win.


Chance Donnelly appeared about an hour before racetime. Short enough that I had to look down on him, he was wiry and slender like jockeys are supposed to be — but he was also arrogant, and I didn't know if that was also how jockeys were supposed to be or not. But I took an instant dislike to him, and it was mutual.

With a dark glance at me but without a word, he circled Pride, looking at him critically. Finally, he said in a short tone of voice, "Heard you let him run out this morning. Word's out in the weight room."

I didn't answer, because there seemed nothing to say.

"Fool thing to do," he went on.

"Somebody spooked the horse," I shot back.

"And my mother's the Queen of England," he said wryly. "Why would anybody spook the horse in morning exercises?"

I couldn't say that I thought T. Joe had done it to give me away as a fake. "Maybe to tire Pride out so he won't run well this afternoon."

"They may have succeeded," he said dryly. "Horse looks all right. We'll see this afternoon. See you in the paddock."

I would never, I thought with regret, ask Chance Donnelly if he knew Bobby Shaw.


"He thought I did it on purpose," I told Benjie angrily.

"Calm down," he replied, "you'll upset your horse."

We were leading Pride toward the paddock. All morning, I'd been talking to Pride about how he was going to win the race. "Don't listen to Chance," I said as I brushed, "just run the best you can. You'll win, I know you will."

Whether or not Pride was in a state of high excitement for the race, I surely was.

Chance, wearing silks in Ferguson's purple and white colors, waited for us in the midst of a group of jockeys who all turned to stare at me as we approached. Obviously, as Chance had said, the story of Pride's runaway had made the rounds — with me as the dumb stable boy who had let it happen. I thought of sticking out my tongue at Chance. Without a word to me, he took Pride's reins and began to saddle the horse. But then he stopped to stare at Benjie.

"You know what goes on around here. Watch out for him." He nodded toward me, obviously the "him" he referred to.

I couldn't decide if Chance meant "watch out for" as in "take care of" or "be sure he doesn't do anything else wrong." Either way, my dislike for the jockey escalated.

As Benjie led me to the fence where we could watch the race, I said conversationally, "I told Pride just to ignore Chance and run the best race he can."

He doubled over with laughter. "You what? Told him to ignore his jockey? Good thing all that horse knows is that you were making noises at him. If he follows your advice, we're in severe trouble."

"Of course he'll follow my advice," I said, never doubting for a minute that Pride understood every word I said. "Besides, Pride knows how to run the race better than that Chance person."

"That Chance person," Benjie mimicked, "is a world-class jockey, and he knows how to run a race — when to let the horse go, how to hold him back in the early part of the race, how to watch out for other horses. He's not just a stick figure up there, riding once around the track, you know." His tone had become scornful.

No, I didn't know, I thought angrily, but I wasn't about to tell Benjie. I lifted my chin in the air and stared at the lineup of waiting horses.

"Here," Benjie said, "try these." He produced a small

pair of binoculars. When I looked through them, I could see the grim expression on Chance Donnelly's face.

Silently, I whispered, "Run, Pride, run your very best." I was sure Pride knew I was talking to him. If you didn't believe in a little magic about horse racing, I thought, it would be boring just watching faraway horses who all looked a miniature blur.

The horses waited, bunched at the gate, while one jockey rode in tight circles on a fractious horse that wouldn't get into its stall. "Texas Jim," Benjie said, "the favorite. Runs like a son-of-a-gun once you get him started, but he's a mess at the gate."

Finally, they got Texas Jim settled outside the gates and the race could begin. They all got away to a clean, fast start, and to my joy, Pride was leading the pack within seconds. "Look, look," I shouted, poking Benjie hard, "he's leading."

"It's too soon," Benjie muttered. "He'll lose his strength. What's the matter with Donnelly?"

"Oh, leave off," I said. "Pride knows what he's doing." I emphasized my words by poking Benjie in the side again.

"Ow!" he yelped, raising a hand as though to cuff me, and then lowering it slowly.

"It's all right," I said, "I'm Caleb. You can hit back."

He grinned, and we both turned our attention back to the horses, who were now thundering around the last turn.

"Pride's still winning!" I shouted.

"Lower your voice, Caleb," Benjie said. "You sound like a girl."

I was too busy watching through the binoculars to pay attention. Pride kept his lead and crossed the finish line almost a full length before the next horse.

"It's Poco's Sweet Pride by a length," boomed the announcer, his voice almost lost to me as I pounded Benjie on the back, demanding, "Did you see? Did you? He heard me! I know he did!"

"Calm down, uh, Caleb, calm down," Benjie said, but there was a bit of laughter in his voice.

40

I waited impatiently while Chance met Ker in the winners' circle. At last, he brought Pride to the paddock where I waited to walk him and cool him down. Benjie had told me that was my next responsibility.

"Guess the run this morning didn't hurt, did it?" I said, unable to resist the temptation.

In spite of his win, Chance was no happier. "Craziest thing I ever saw," he said, his tone somehow artificial, as though he wanted his reaction on record. "I tried to hold him back, save for the homestretch, but he ran away on me."

"Glad I'm not the only one he does that too," I said, taking the reins out of his hands.

"You give him elephant juice?" he asked suspiciously.

I thought the man had taken leave of his senses. What was elephant juice? And why would I give it to Pride? I turned away without a word, though I heard him still talking as Pride and I walked away.

Ker Ferguson was ecstatic. "Pride, you're living up to your name." Beside himself with joy, he threw his arms around the horse's neck. "I told them you could do it," he triumphed.

"Told who?" I asked curiously, before I remembered that family back on the ranch who disapproved of racing.

"What? Oh, nothing." Ker suddenly looked like he'd spoken out of turn.

But I knew — or thought I did. In my mind, I could see his stern, disapproving family as though they watched the race over his shoulder and frowned when Pride won. This time, in my mind, his mother looked a lot like Mrs. Wiley Langdon.

"Thanks, Caleb," he said, interrupting my fantasy. "You've done a fine job with Pride. He doesn't race again for almost a week, so we can kind of take it easy. Tomorrow the track's closed — Sunday, of course. I'll feed and water Pride. See you Monday."

"Ker?" I asked. "What's elephant juice?"

His eyes narrowed. "One way of doping a horse," he

said cautiously. "Hops 'em up so they'll run their darn-edest, even if they're in pain. Why?"

"Chance accused me of giving it to Pride," I said, indignation written all over my face.

I expected him to ask if I had done that or be worried about the possibility or something, but I was totally unprepared for Ker Ferguson's reaction. He laughed aloud, a great roaring sound that bespoke real amusement.

When he finally had himself under control again, he said, "That really is ridiculous. You — of all people! I'll have to tell Chance you didn't even know what he was talking about." And he limped off, whistling cheerily.

As I closed the stall door for the night, I caught T. Joe watching me, while trying hard to ignore me. "Hey, T. Joe," I said in my deepest voice.

"You remember what I said," he answered. "When something happens to that horse . . ."

"Get out of here, T. Joe," I said, advancing toward him with my fists clenched, showing a bravado that I didn't feel.

To my great relief, he turned and fled.

Benjie came up. "You threaten T. Joe?" he asked with a grin. Then, "You collect your winnings?"

"No," I said, "I didn't bet." It was silly, I had told myself, to let Aunt Edna's fears dictate to me. Yet, I was reluctant to place that second bet.

"Last chance to earn really good money," he said, shaking his head. "Odds are going down. He'll be a favorite, now that he's won a race. More people bet on favorites, so there's not as much for any one winner."

"And this time he was a longshot?" I knew that because Benjie had told me, but I didn't know what it meant.

Benjie grinned. "You're learning. Golly Gee was a longshot day before yesterday, and lots of money was bet on him at the last, 'cause word got around he'd surprise everybody. But Pride was the surprise today."

"Does Mr. Bertelli own Golly Gee?" I asked, still curious about all the intricate relationships at a racetrack.

"Naw, he trains him for a Mr. Burke . . . trains four

42

other horses here too. Ker's unusual, being owner and trainer both and having only one horse." Then he grinned. "Pride's unusual too. He's no longshot — he's a winner."

"Yes," I smiled, "he really is."

Pride, I learned when the stable boys gathered for their evening chat, was a real surprise to everyone. He'd not been expected to show at all.

"He runs again, somebody'll be after him, you watch and see," Lonnie said. Though it was spoken lightheartedly, I heard a deadly warning in the words that sent chills up my spine. I remembered T. Joe's ominous words.

"After him?" I echoed the words before I thought.

Lonnie looked pityingly at me. "There's them that don't like a surprise in racing," he said slowly, "and they got the power to enforce it."

"Oh, sure," I said, trying to sound casual.

Tired as I was, I trailed behind Benjie when he went to collect his bet — he'd made twenty-three dollars on a two-dollar bet, just like I had the day before, and he was planning to give every penny of it to his mother. His surprise when I asked if he wasn't going to hold a little back made me feel like two cents.

"Of course not," he said, "Ma needs the money worse than I do. And she can cook a lot better than I can," he added with a smile.

There was an endless row of sellers' windows under the main grandstand. A great commotion greeted us as we approached — yelling, screaming, shouting, all of it joyful sounding. Once we rounded a corner and entered the betting area, we saw a huge, unruly mob. Some people danced, others laughed and slapped their neighbors on the back heartily, some just waved their hands in the air triumphantly. At the center of it seemed to be a small, middle-aged couple, dressed almost as poorly as I had been the first day of racing, the woman in a homemade cotton dress, the man in scuffed boots and worn Levis. They smiled rather self-consciously at each other, then at the hilarity around them, then back at each other. A guard stood next to them, watching the crowd

43

and watching, in particular, the small canvas bag the man clutched tightly to his body.

"Winners," Benjie breathed, "big winners."

The story was in the newspaper the next day. A Mr. and Mrs. Frank Edgerton of Alvarado had been about to lose their farm, which had been in the family for two generations, because they hadn't been able to pay the mortgage, just like Uncle Charlie and his store. Before taking off to California like everyone else, they decided to make one last desperate gamble. They took their life savings — $1,000 hidden in a pillowcase in their house — and bet it on Poco's Sweet Pride. They won enough money to pay off their mortgage in full, with some left over.

"Why that horse?" a reporter asked, and Mrs. Edgerton answered, "I just liked the name."

"Aunt Edna," I said when she showed me the article, "you can't say that was the devil. Look at what racing did for those poor, deserving people." Secretly, I was proud that it was Pride who'd won the money for them.

"Twenty more will be ruined because of it," she said bitterly. "They'll all think the same thing can happen to them, and there will be hordes of the ignorant betting their life savings."

"Of course there won't," I said. "Most people are too smart for that." I didn't know how soon I was to learn that her words were right and that people weren't always as smart as I gave them credit for.

# Chapter 4

## The Devil Amongst Us

Aunt Edna didn't much go to church these days — too hard, she said, to get up the aisle. And besides, she didn't feel the Lord had blessed her lately. Sunday found her, though, sitting in her chair, reading her Bible.

I dressed for church, then snuck back out to the shed and grabbed the garments that had become my work clothes. After two days, they badly needed washing, but I could hardly scrub them on the board in the kitchen, where Aunt Edna would no doubt find me. And I couldn't take them to the laundress at Mrs. Langdon's, that's for sure. I took them to a friend's home.

"Callie!" Frankie Gambrell's surprise was genuine. I'd seen her only occasionally since I'd left school and gone to Mrs. Langdon's, but we always picked up where we left off. Her family was as poor as mine, and her parents were good friends of Uncle Charlie and Aunt Edna, although Aunt Edna, being so reclusive of late, had lost touch with them. Still, in a way, they were the closest thing I had to relatives.

Now, I was too involved in the problem of my dirty clothes to look closely at Frankie. If I had, I'd have seen red-rimmed eyes with a tight, scared look, her face pale, her short brown hair not as neatly combed as usual. She held the door open only a bit, certainly not inviting me in. Beyond her, I saw the familiar shabby living room, an afghan thrown across the sofa to cover its loose threads. The drapes were pulled, and the house was dark and silent.

"I . . . I need to wash out some clothes, and I can't do it at home, and it's a long story . . . can I wash my clothes here?"

The Frankie I knew would have laughed and demanded the whole story, but she just said, "Here?"

Then I looked at her. "Frankie?"

She looked over her shoulder, then stepped out the door, and whispered, "It's Pa. He's been gambling at the racetrack, and he lost Ma's grocery money. She owes down to Mr. Luckett's market, and now she can't pay it. And Mr. Luckett — he said no more credit."

"He lost at the racetrack?" I echoed.

"Yeah. Promised Ma he wouldn't bet, wouldn't even go near the track, but he came home last night without a penny in his pocket. Ma's frantic." She bit her lip.

"What'd he say?" I expected to hear that he'd been drunk and not in control of himself, but such wasn't the case at all.

She threw her hands up in the air and walked in a small circle of frustration on the stoop where we stood. "He cried. Said he couldn't help himself. Says he doesn't know what made him do it."

"The devil," I muttered.

"What?"

"Nothing. I . . . Aunt Edna says racing is the devil's work, and I never believed her."

"Don't much believe in the devil myself," she said, "but your aunt could be right this time. I . . . I don't think this is a good time for you to wash your clothes, Callie. Ma's too upset to have anyone else in the house."

We talked about this and that for a few minutes — Frankie's pa was out of work and her ma did day work,

46

but there was little of that these days. Frankie had been lucky. She clerked at a five-and-dime, but her pay was not enough to support them, and besides, she said, she saw a grim life stretching endlessly out before her unless something changed.

"Pa says we'll pull up and go to California, but me . . . I think I'll go to Dallas *alone*," she said.

When she asked about Mrs. Langdon and I told her about the racetrack and Ker Ferguson, Frankie's eyes narrowed. "How can you work there?" she asked angrily. "How can you be part of taking people's money?"

"I'm not part of that," I said defensively, wanting to add that no one "took" her pa's money. He'd given it willingly — apparently too willingly.

"You're part of it. Without you, the horses wouldn't race, and people couldn't bet." And with that, Frankie, who'd been so quiet, turned and went inside, slamming the door behind her and leaving me clutching my dirty clothes.

"Some people win," I said angrily at the closed door. It would have been cruel to tell her about the Edgertons.

I ended up hiding my clothes in the shed, searching Uncle Charlie's trunk for more pants and shirts, and, finally, washing my clothes at the stables the next day. Ker Ferguson never asked a thing about it, but Benjie was unmerciful.

"Wash mine too? Maybe you could take in laundry, if you don't learn to ride any better." He was terribly amused at his joke.

I'd stayed on Pride at morning exercises and I hadn't let him run away with me, but the difference between my riding and Benjie's was painfully obvious. And the painful part was real — I was stiff and sore from my runaway ride on Saturday, and this morning I'd developed blisters in places I didn't want to talk about.

"Watch the races?" Benjie asked in the early afternoon. Golly Gee wasn't racing that day, and neither was Pride.

"No," I said shortly, resentment still strong in me over his jokes about my laundry and, worse, about my riding.

"Good," he said firmly. "You stay here and sulk. I'm going to bet and win some money . . . find the right girl, I might buy her supper with my winnings."

"You do that," I said, fixing my attention on the harness I was polishing. It took effort not to look at him. *Darn you, Benjie,* I thought, *you treat me like a girl, and I like it. How can I ever convince everyone else I'm a boy?*

Ker came along about that time. "Caleb," he said, "you've been working too hard. Go watch the races with Benjie. But don't lose your wages betting."

Since he hadn't paid me any wages yet, that wouldn't be hard.

"Here, give me your two dollars, and I'll bet for you too," Benjie said. "Gonna put our money on Millsdale's Sweet Sue." It never occurred to him that I might resent his taking over my money, my thoughts.

"I'm not betting," I said.

"Not betting? You won good money the other day."

"I'm not going to bet again," I said firmly. "It gets to be a compulsion . . . it's probably worse if you win than if you lose." I gave him what I meant to be a long, serious look.

Instead of being properly reprimanded, Benjie broke into laughter. "Compulsion? Where'd you get that word? Your aunt whatever-her-name-is?"

I stayed silent, not willing to tell him about Frankie and her father.

"I guess you mean it," he said, shaking his head in bewilderment. "You've got your chin up in the air again, the way you do when you don't want to talk about something." With that, he walked away, leaving me to lower my chin deliberately and wonder how I gave myself away.

I was standing by the track at one end of the main grandstand. A black Ford, fanciest car I'd ever seen, honked as it pulled right up to the fence, warning me to move on or be run over. "Hey!" I cried indignantly.

48

"Move on, boy," said the uniformed driver. "This is Colonel Waggoner's spot." He pulled the car up sideways, stopped the motor, and got out to open one back door.

I waited curiously to see Colonel Waggoner emerge, but nothing happened. Then, from the depths of the back of the car, came an inquisitive voice, "Who you talking to, Tom?"

"One of the stable boys got in my way," the driver said offhandedly. "No problem."

"Let me talk to him," came the voice, just as I turned away to look for Benjie.

"You there," the driver demanded. "Mr. Waggoner wants to talk to you." It was like a summons from above, clearly not to be ignored, though the driver's expression was fraught with diapproval.

"Me?" Darn! My voice squeaked again.

"You! Get over here!"

I did as I was told and approached the back of the automobile, sticking my head through the open door. A shrunken old man sat in there, a red plaid robe across his knees, a gray fedora on his head, and dark glasses covering his eyes. His fingers tapped restlessly on the carved wooden cane he held in one hand.

"You wanted me, sir?" I asked, awe and surprise making me polite. This was W. T. Waggoner, the man who owned the Three-D Farms and Arlington Downs, the man who owned the second biggest ranch in all of Texas.

"What horse you take care of?" His voice was surprisingly strong for such a frail body.

"Poco's Sweet Pride," I answered.

He nodded, and a lopsided smile lightened the tightness of his aged face. "A winner, I hear." He nodded to himself, and after a fairly long silence I thought I was dismissed. Just as I was about to turn away, he asked, "Boy? You like the races?"

"Don't know much about them, sir. But I like the horses." There seemed no point in telling him about the Edgertons and Frankie's pa and the moral complexities all those stories raised.

49

"Most exciting sport in all the world," he said. "I can't see 'em anymore" — he gestured toward his eyes, and I realized that the dark glasses bespoke blindness — "but I can hear 'em. It's the only thing I look forward to anymore — hearing those horse come 'round the track."

"Yessir," I said. I'd been sure that a man as rich as Colonel Waggoner raced horses for the money, his eye always on the profit, and yet, here he was telling me that racing was a passion, not a business, for him.

"Here," he said, reaching in his pocket, "you go bet this on Cowpuncher's Boy for me. He wins, you keep the money and remember that Pappy gave it to you." He held out two crumpled dollars.

Gingerly, I took the money. "Yessir. If he wins, I'll bring the money back to you."

"No!" The strong voice rose in anger now. "Got all the money I need. It's the thrill of it. You, on the other hand, need the money. You keep it."

"Thank you, Colonel Waggoner," I managed. "Good day to you. I've enjoyed talking to you."

The only answer was a kind of cackle. The driver frowned at me as I left.

Benjie was still in the betting line, and I slid in ahead of him. When I put two dollars on Cowpuncher's Boy, he yowled indignantly. "First of all, you don't bet, remember? And second, that's a dumb bet. That horse is *not* going to win."

"I'm betting for Colonel Waggoner," I said sweetly and turned and left. He followed me up to the top of the stands.

Benjie was right. Cowpuncher's Boy trailed badly, fourth out of the gate and losing ground steadily after that. I didn't mind not winning the money myself, but I ached a little for Mr. Waggoner. I really wanted his horse to win, just so he could have the thrill, not the money.

On the way back to the stables, we wandered through the crowd and came near the gate where the attendant tried to stop me the first day. Just outside the gate the same prophet of doom was broadcasting his message about Sodom and Gomorrah, but no one paid any attention. The crowd parted around him, like a herd of cattle will part around a tree in a pasture, and then went on. But while I watched, Ker came by and, to my amazement, stopped, spoke to the man, and then handed him a dollar. I shook my head. Ker Ferguson was hard to figure out.

When I got back to the stables, the lower half of Pride's stall door was open. I could see it as I rounded the corner of the building, and I knew Ker wasn't there. Hadn't I just seen him? Leaving a speechless Benjie to trail behind, I took off at a dead run, bursting into the stall so breathless that I could scarce talk.

Mr. Bertelli stood there, one hand in a pocket, the other resting gently on Pride's flank. The horse was breathing heavily, nervous and upset.

"What," I demanded breathlessly, "are you doing here?"

He tried to assume a scornful look. "Just looking at this longshot that suddenly became a winner," he said. But something in his tone struck me as nervous . . . or guilty . . . or both.

"You're not supposed to be in the stall of another trainer's horse," I said, my breath caught enough that I could pitch my voice low.

"Is that a law?" He had taken his hand off Pride, but he seemed determined to keep the other hand in his pocket, as though he were clutching something.

"I understand," I said calmly, "that it's an unwritten rule . . . a courtesy, if you will."

"Maybe," he muttered, brushing past me. "I don't believe in foolish courtesies." He smelled of garlic.

It took me almost a full hour to calm Pride down. Finally, I simply walked him back and forth in front of the stables, until the exercise pushed the willies out of him. Every time I walked by Golly Gee's stall, I sensed Mr. Bertelli staring darkly at me, and once I saw Benjie cast a furtive glance my way. But he was busy with his own chores — and probably, friend or no, not about to jeopardize his job for my sake, or for Pride's.

51

As I walked I tried to puzzle out why Mr. Bertelli would have been in the stall — and, more important, why he looked so guilty. And should I tell Ker? In the long run, I decided not to tell him, figuring that I'd simply give myself away as a nervous greenhorn.

I locked the stall door carefully that night when I left. Benjie was nowhere to be seen, and I missed him. I didn't know if I'd have asked him about his boss or not, but it dawned on me that I was getting used to Benjie's company.

The main gate of the racetrack fronted on U.S. Highway 80, the major highway that went all the way from North Texas to California, or so they told me. I'd never been farther west than Fort Worth, some fifteen miles beyond Arlington, but sometimes I used to watch the cars head westward and think about driving to California to find my father.

Lately, the cars that headed west were rickety, often rusty old pickups, loaded with household goods. It was downright sad to see someone's life tied to the back of a pickup with baling wire — a worn couch, perhaps a battered chest of drawers, sometimes a sewing machine, a well-used rocking horse, all kinds of things that told you what kind of folks had packed up their lives and headed for California. Once I'd seen a birdcage, but there was no bird in it.

As I swung through the gate this night, I saw that one of those trucks, piled with furniture and people, had broken down by the side of the road. Three small children — a boy in ragged coveralls, a girl in a dirty cotton dress, and a child young enough to wear diapers — stood watching while a man in coveralls and no shirt fiddled with a steaming engine. Beside them stood a worn and tired-looking woman clutching a tiny infant.

There was not a thing I could do to help them, but I

went over to the truck anyway. "Car trouble?" I asked, sensing the stupidity of the obvious question.

"Guess it ran out of oil. Threw a rod," the man said, slamming the hood in disgust. He looked around in despair, as though he'd been hoping that shelter for his family would magically appear on the roadside. Then, for the first time apparently, he saw the racetrack.

"Gollee! What in tarnation is that place?"

"Arlington Downs," I told him. "Horse racing."

The woman and children stood silent, watchful and wary, while their father said to me, "You mean folks got the money to race horses?"

"Yeah," I said, studying the horizon so I didn't have to look at him.

"You race horses?" he asked, and it occurred to me he would believe almost anything I told him. I resisted the urge to present myself as a famous jockey and said, instead, "I'm a stable boy. I muck out stables."

That reassured him enough that he offered his hand. "Name's Russell," he said, "Jimmy Don Russell. Pleased to meet you."

"Cal . . ." I almost did it again. "Caleb Shaw," I said, taking the rough hand and wishing I still had my gloves on, though my own soft hands had toughened considerably in the last few days.

"That's my wife, Ada, and these here are John-boy, Sara Sue, and Jessie. The baby's Nathan." Ragged or no, he swelled with pride as he introduced his family.

I shook hands with the children, smiled at his wife, and made noises about being glad to know them. "You folks need some food?"

"We got some jerky," the woman said softly, "and some fruit. Don't want to be beholden."

"Where you from?" I asked.

"Lonesome Dove," the father said, and then grew suddenly defensive. "Had a good farm there, nice home. Drought ruined it all."

"We're goin' to California," said the boy, who looked to

53

be no more than seven, though Lord knows I was no judge of children and their ages. "Pa says it's a golden land."

"Yes," I said softly, almost forgetting my disguise, "I think it is." Then, looking at the father again and lowering into my Caleb voice, I asked, "Where you folks gonna stay tonight?"

The father shrugged and pointed to the car. I opened my mouth to say I'd take them home, but a quick vision of Aunt Edna stopped the words. She'd been known to share our sparse meals a time or two when a hungry stranger showed up at the door, but to invite a whole family to spend the night was a far different matter. Still, poor as Aunt Edna and I were, we'd never been faced with sleeping by the side of the road or eating jerky. Something wouldn't let me walk away from these people.

"There's a mattress in the back," the man said. "We'll make do."

"I . . . I'll bring you some provisions in the morning," I said lamely.

"Caleb!" The voice came from behind me, and I turned to see Ker limping toward me. His pickup — new and shiny, compared to the Russells' — was pulled up behind me. "What's the problem?"

"These folks' car broke down, sir," I said. "They're gonna sleep right here by the side of the road."

"Of course they're not!" he said swiftly, and my heart sank. Had I underestimated him? Was he going to forbid them to stop here on a public road?

"I have a small house — but a big barn, and you're welcome to bed down there. Be pleased to have you."

Jimmy Don Russell looked at Ada, and then at me, and then at Ker. "We don't want to be beholden . . . ."

"Nonsense," Ker said. "Man can't let his wife and children sleep on a public road. Get what you need, and then get in." He motioned toward his truck.

"Our things?" Ada asked nervously.

"Trust in the Lord," Jimmy Don said. "We've had to do that so far, and he's watched over us, ain't he?" He nodded toward Ker.

"Caleb," Ker asked, "you need a ride?"

"No, thanks," I said. I stood rooted to the spot until they drove away, the children silent and staring, Jimmy Don awkwardly sitting in the front with Ker, who honked at me as he pulled out.

Then I turned and headed for Aunt Edna, more grateful than I'd ever been for our tiny home — and even for squash for dinner.

Jimmy Don and his family stayed the night with Ker, who got their truck fixed and headed them toward Califiornia the next day.

"You pay for the repairs?" I asked boldly.

"None of your business," he told me, which meant that he had paid.

"Pride better win again and make you some money," I said, half-joking.

Things went along without incident that quiet week. I grew better at morning exercises, and I began to feel more and more like Caleb, though Benjie still called me "Callie" every chance he got, and I knew he did it deliberately.

On Wednesday and Thursday, the races were fairly predictable, with favorites winning most of the time. But on Friday, a longshot named Robertson's Bright Future won big. He was one of the horses Bertelli trained.

"Bet your boss is pleased, huh?" I said to Benjie conversationally.

"He's not the only one," he said, but I was surprised at the bitterness in his tone.

"What's the matter?" We were sitting on a bale of straw outside the stables, taking a breather from mucking out stalls and cleaning tack.

"Somebody bet a lot of money on Bright Future, just before the betting closed," he said. "They're gonna ruin racing, ruin Pappy Waggoner's dream."

"Benjie Thompson," I demanded, "what're you talking about?"

55

"Never mind," he said gruffly, "but you watch Pride. Someone may be angry that he came from behind like he did." And then he got up, leaving me sitting there stewing.

I reported the conversation to Ker, who told me to ignore it. "I don't want to believe races are fixed and all that," he said. "Bright Future won fair and square. So did Pride."

Something told me that Ker was too trusting, and that Benjie was more realistic.

My view was confirmed when Pride ran the next week. He was spirited at morning exercises, and I held the reins tight to avoid another runaway. "Don't worry, Pride," I told him, "you'll get your chance to run like the wind this afternoon. Just run like you want to, not like Chance wants you to."

He twitched his ears at my voice, and I knew he understood.

Chance was a little more friendly when I delivered Pride to the paddock this time, but that didn't make him more likeable. "Didn't run a blowout this morning, did you?" he asked, in a poor attempt at a joke.

"Naw," I said, "I left that for you."

He patted Pride familiarly and dismissed me with a curt nod. Benjie was nowhere to be seen, so I went off to check the betting on the tote board. Pride was the favorite in this race, with odds only two-to-one, but there seemed to be a lot of last-minute activity at the betting windows. The tote board, calculated and filled in by hand, couldn't keep up.

I ran into Ker, who said, "Heavy money's bet on Pride, including some of my own."

"He'll win again," I assured him and together we went to the fence to watch the race.

The horses all lined up at the gate in reasonably good order, and they all got away to a clean start. Pride left the gate fifth in the pack, and even without binoculars I could tell from the first that he was not doing well, running calmly in the middle of the pack, with no sign of surging ahead.

56

"Chance's holding him back, like he should," Ker said, but I detected a note of worry in his voice. By the homestretch, Pride had edged up to fourth, out of a field of twelve, and I totally forgot who I was, screaming at the top of my lungs for Pride to "come on home."

Ker ignored the race for one long moment while he looked at me and said, with genuine amazement, "You're a girl!"

I was too wrapped up in the race for it even to register what had happened. "Pride," I yelled at him, "Pride's not winning."

Pride came in sixth. A longshot named Fast Fellow surged out of the pack just lengths from the finish line to win by a head.

"He didn't run right," I said to Ker, "something was wrong out there."

"Nonsense. Pride just lost the race." But Ker's disappointment was evident in his eyes, which didn't twinkle as usual, and in his bearing — he didn't have that jauntiness that usually carried him from place to place, and his limp was more pronounced as we walked toward the paddock.

An impatient, angry Chance waited for us. "He ran like mush," he said. "Sluggish, wouldn't — no, *couldn't* — respond to what I wanted him to do. Look at his eyes!"

I looked at Pride and instead of bright, curious eyes, I saw dullness, an almost sleepy look. "What's wrong with him?" I asked, my voice rising in anxiety.

"He's been doped, bet you anything," Chance said, and then turned on me accusingly. "You been watching him? You leave him alone in the stall today?"

"No," I said, searching my memory. "Not at all . . . . well, I went to get water, and I . . . I talked to Benjie, but we were right outside."

"Somebody got to this horse," Chance said with finality. "Somebody who wanted Fast Fellow to win."

"Who trains Fast Fellow?" Ker asked.

"Bertelli," was the answer which sent my mind reeling.

"Caleb," Ker said, "you best walk Pride and cool him

down." And then, I could tell by the expression on his face, he remembered my high-pitched scream during the race. "And then wait for me in his stall. We . . . we have to talk."

I walked away, leaving Ker and Chance in deep discussion, and taking with me my confusion about Pride's race and the dead certainty that it would not be my business much longer anyway. Ker Ferguson would give me the sack.

# Chapter 5

# The Truth Revealed

Guilt and truth — or the lack of it — rolled into one great lump in my throat as I walked Pride up and down. This time, the walking was less to cool him than it was to keep him moving and work whatever he'd been given out of his system.

As I walked I took all the blame: If I hadn't lied about being a girl and about knowing about horses, Ker would have gotten a stable boy who knew what he was doing, Pride never would have been doped, and Ker would have had a winner. The longer Pride and I walked, the guiltier I felt. First I break a piece of carnival glass, then I ruin a valuable racehorse's career. What next? I wondered.

Finally, Ker came along, his limping step having recovered some but not all of its usual jauntiness. "Bring him in the stall," he said, his tone neither friendly nor short.

I followed, my mouth open to tell him that I'd leave, he'd never see me again, I was only waiting to hand Pride over to his capable hands. But he spoke before I could get a word out.

"Why did you tell me you were a boy?"

I stole a look at his face, expecting anger, and found, instead, amusement, which gave me a little courage. "Would you have hired a girl?" I asked.

He thought about that. "No, probably not."

"But I lied to you," I said in a rush, "I don't know enough about horses to take care of Pride — "

He shrugged. "I knew that all along, never doubted it, but you seemed willing and honest . . . better than boys I've had before who know a whole lot about horses and too much about racetracks. Only thing was — I remember looking at your hands . . ." His voice trailed off.

"It's my fault — "

"You can wallow in pity if you want," he said, "but I got more on my mind than that. I'm going to make public what happened to Pride, and I'm going to apply for a third race for him."

"Third race?"

"Another lesson for you, Cal . . . what is your name?"

"Callie," I said, "short for Calpurnia."

"And nobody ever calls you Calpurnia, right?"

I nodded. I really liked this man who stood before me, even if he wasn't tall and handsome and red-haired — and I hadn't heard him sing yet. "The third race?" I prompted.

"Can't run a horse too often. Racing's real hard on 'em, and today was to have been Pride's last race this season — it was his second, after all. But he . . . I . . . we . . . all of us got cheated, and well, he's a tough horse . . . I really believe that he can run a third time."

"Chance?" I asked, knowing the jockey would have an opinion.

"Chance said it's the dumbest idea he ever heard, but there are other jockeys."

"And other stable boys," I said. "I'll be going, but I want . . . well, I'm really sorry I ruined things for you."

"Whoa, Calpurnia!" Now he was laughing. "You're not going anywhere. You're in this with me. Pride trusts you . . . and so do I. This could have happened to anybody, and probably would have happened sooner if Benjie

60

hadn't run Willie off. No, our problem is do we keep up your disguise, or do we tell the world you're a girl?"

I was speechless, so speechless I sat down, hard, on the hay and my cap tumbled off, releasing my hair.

Ker looked at me a long minute and then said, "That must be an omen. You'll be Calpurnia from now on."

"No," I said louder than I meant, "Callie. Never Calpurnia."

Then, to my surprise, he handed me twenty dollars. "Here, this is your pay for the first week."

It wasn't like winning on a bet, but it was sure more than Mrs. Langdon ever paid me in a month. I'd give every penny of it to Aunt Edna this time.

T. Joe was the first to shout, "I told you so, I told you so," when I tried to stroll — casually — to the water spigot, my cap gone and my hair caught at the back of my neck to keep it out of my face.

"I told you you were a girl!" he said triumphantly.

"I already knew it," I replied. "Didn't need you to tell me."

"Could have fooled me," Walter said, his face an open book of amazement. "Wow! Wait till I tell my ma, she'll have a wall-eyed fit at somebody being so unladylike."

I threw him a withering look, but it sailed over the top of that big dumb head.

Lonnie was more reserved in his comments. "I thought there was something," he said, "but I didn't know what. My hat's off to you . . . you pulled it off right well."

Benjie just watched me from a distance, without a word, and I wondered about his reaction. He'd always treated me like Callie, and now that my identity was public, I wanted him to recognize that . . . oh, I didn't know, but I was infuriated that he said nothing, did nothing, just stood there, staring in that way of his.

It was Mr. Bertelli, naturally, who raised the roof.

61

"Who is she?" he demanded loudly, and Benjie said something soft to him.

"You're kidding!" Bertelli said, and then, just as loudly, "Not for long, she isn't." He took off in great long strides toward Pride's stall, where Ker stood watching the whole scene.

I got my pail of water and headed back to the stall, but stopped at a good piece away, figuring discretion was the better part of — what was it Aunt Edna always said? Anyway, I stopped where I could hear the conversation, yet wasn't right up on top of them.

Bertelli was waving his arms and yelling, "You can't let her stay here, Ferguson. I told you he . . . she . . . whoever . . . was trouble, and now I can prove it. She's a girl, a damn girl!"

Ker looked amused. "Yes, Bertelli, she is, and a fine one too."

"She can't stay," Bertelli repeated. "She'll cause all kinds of trouble . . . the lads will be fighting over her. She can't ride a horse . . . she —"

"She stays," Ker said calmly.

Bertelli clenched his fist and backed off a little, as though he were going to take a swing at Ker, who simply stood his ground and stared. Then, the irate trainer seemed to get hold of himself. "I've got a lot riding on this season," he said intensely, "and I won't have some dither-headed girl messing it up for me." He threw me a threatening look and strode off.

When I came up to him, Ker said, "I think you've made an enemy . . . and not one that I take lightly. He's the kind that'll rustle your cattle at night."

"What?"

"That's what my father always says about untrustworthy cowboys on the ranch. Guess it applies here too."

Ker's parents came the next day from the ranch outside Brownwood where they raised sheep and cattle —

an unlikely but profitable combination. He found them waiting at his house that night and told me about it the next morning when he arrived at the stables.

"Heard about the win, they did," he said gloomily, "and came to talk to me about it."

Now, Ker had never told me about his parents' attitude — I'd only heard it from Benjie — so I pretended not to understand his glum mood. "Are they celebrating?" I asked brightly.

"Not hardly," was the reply. "They think they should make one more attempt to talk me out of racing, before I get in any deeper, as they put it."

Visions of the *American Gothic* couple danced in my head again.

"They . . . I'm taking them to lunch in the clubhouse, because I thought it would show them how respectable racing is — it's so posh and all," he said miserably. "But now I don't know if that's a good idea . . . may just reinforce their disapproval of gambling, seeing so many people living comfortably when the rest of the world is in desperate straits."

He paused a minute and then seemed to have an enlightened idea. "Callie," he said tentatively, as though he were still testing out my new identity, "why don't you have lunch with us?"

"Me? Oh, no, no thank you, Ker. I couldn't . . . well, you see, I'm not dressed for it." I looked down at my jeans and the voluminous man's shirt I had tried unsuccessfully to tuck in, its huge sleeves rolled to my elbows. After the workout of morning exercises — a workout for horse and rider alike — my face glistened with perspiration, and my hair hung in damp tendrils. "No," I said once more, for emphasis.

He never heard a word I said. "Yes, you'd divert some of their displeasure. You go home and change into a dress . . . meet us back here at the stall at noon."

"Ker! I can't . . . I don't have . . . ." I didn't really want to say I didn't have anything to wear besides a worn cotton dress or my one good dress. I paused, realizing how much I wanted to see inside the clubhouse. That two-story brick structure, sitting imposingly next to the grandstand, had drawn my eye so that even Benjie had teased me about it and then advised me, seriously, to forget any notions of going inside. "It's not for the likes of us," he had said.

"No argument," Ker said. "I'll tend to Pride this morning." And then he was gone before I could protest anymore.

I thought about looking for Benjie, lately my answer to every problem. But what, really, could Benjie have told me that I couldn't tell myself?

So I went home, mystifying Aunt Edna. I pacified her with some vague explanation that I'd spilled food on my dress.

"You're wearing your best dress to wait tables?" she asked suspiciously as I slipped into a green faille dress with a wonderfully full skirt that she had made for me, protesting the skirt's yards of material all the while.

"Just this once, Aunt Edna," I assured her. "Big dignitaries coming to the clubhouse today." Well, special people, anyway, I thought. And I went away, singing about Loch Lomond as I walked back to the track.


And that's how I found myself sitting at a fine table in the clubhouse, dressed in the only good dress I owned, with shoes that pinched, and a determined smile plastered on my face.

All visions of "American Gothic" had vanished the minute I met the Fergusons. Mr. Ferguson was a West Texas rancher, no doubt about that — his Stetson was creased and spotted from long use, his worn jeans fit smoothly on legs skinnier than Ker's, and he wore a western-style yoked shirt and scuffed boots, though they looked to be finely made. Mrs. Ferguson was short, slightly dumpy, and wearing a flowered dress that would have delighted Aunt Edna, her gray hair carefully pushed into finger waves. Altogether a middle-class couple, threatening to no one — and not a stern look between them.

Obviously, they adored Ker. Mrs. Ferguson hung onto his arm as we went into the clubhouse, and Mr. Ferguson addressed several questions toward him, always ending with, "Eh, son?"

Where, I wondered, was that unbending couple with their stern disapproval of racing?

I found them at lunch, but not before my eyes fell out of my head at the splendor in the clubhouse. A mustachioed white-coated waiter smoothly seated us at a table for four, overlooking the track.

"Champagne?" he asked.

Before Ker could reply, his father said shortly, "No. Iced tea. For all of us."

"Very good, sir," and the waiter was gone.

"Callie is . . . my stable boy," Ker said, "and I asked her to join us because I thought you'd like to meet her. She's been a big help to me in the last week."

"A girl as a stable boy?" Mrs. Ferguson said, looking closely at me.

I opened my mouth to reply, though I had not one idea of what to say, but Ker said, "It's a long story, Mama. But if you knew Callie, you'd like her."

"I never heard of a girl in a stable," Mrs. Ferguson said, "but I suppose these days people do anything they can, including things that aren't ladylike." Her look to me was pitying rather than critical, but it still made me uncomfortable.

Who, I wondered, did she think she was to criticize me? Had she ever taken in ironing? Or worked for Mrs. Wiley Langdon or the likes? But then I realized Aunt Edna, who had none of Mrs. Ferguson's advantages, would have felt the same way. And besides, Mrs. Ferguson kept looking at me with a smile on her face. Obviously, she was no ogre.

"Is Ker your only child?" I asked brightly, not noticing in time that Ker winced.

"No," Mrs. Ferguson said, her sweet smile never changing. "We have a daughter in Brownwood. She's married to a banker, and they have three children. They all follow the Baptist way." Her look at Ker was slightly accusing.

Fortunately, just then the waiter handed us each menus — great huge pieces of heavy and shiny paper, with long lists of delicacies printed on them, from quail on toast to chocolate mousse.

Though the menu intrigued me beyond belief, I stole a look around the room. Just as I'd imagined that first day at the track, the walls were paneled in rich wood. I wasn't smart enough to know what kind of wood, but I saw and appreciated the glossy deep reddish-brown, the hand-rubbed look. Curtains of red velvet were swagged well back at each window, so as not to block the view of the track. We sat in heavy wooden chairs, with backs and seats upholstered in a heavy ribbed material, and the table before us was covered with white linen. Sparkling footed glasses sat at each plate — even if we didn't have champagne, they were filled with ice water — and heavy silverware framed each place setting.

I thought I'd died and gone to heaven.

And then I thought that Aunt Edna had probably never, ever seen such grandness in all her life. And it struck me as wrong that I was enjoying it. A taste of ash crept into my mouth and stayed there all through the lunch, though I enjoyed a magnificent chicken salad with apples and oranges, fresh popovers that melted in your mouth, and for dessert a chocolate cake of some kind so rich that I thought I might be sick.

Ker asked his parents if they didn't like the sur-roundings — his father replied that they were "just plain people" — and then he pointed out various dignitaries in the room, though how he knew them I could never figure out. Still, I was impressed that he pointed out three state legislators, the mayors of Dallas and Fort Worth, two national senators, and a European prince. The latter, he said, owned a horse that was to race the next day.

None of it made much impression on Mr. Ferguson. As he found out, he had a bone to pick with Ker. "Son," he said, "your horse won."

That, I thought, was a statement of the obvious, and I waited to see what Ker would respond. He, too, was obvious.

"Yes, sir," he said.

"People lost money because he won," the father went on.

"Uh . . . not many," Ker said, his nervousness beginning to show.

"It's wrong, son, just flat wrong." This was delivered without emotion, just a simple statement of what appeared to be a clear fact.

"I know you both feel that way," Ker said, nodding to take his mother into this discussion, "but I don't . . . racing benefits the state. And let me tell you about the couple who won big the other day . . ."

"It doesn't matter who wins and who loses," his father said. "The Bible speaks against it."

As I realized that Ker's father was contradicting his own argument, I began to squirm uncomfortably. Aunt Edna was against betting, but she never quoted the Bible to me — and, somehow, she was never as deadly serious. This plain scared me.

It struck me that Mrs. Ferguson was sitting silent during this whole discussion. Her eyes were fixed tightly on her husband, except for quick, darting glances that she shot toward Ker. At one point, he reached over and covered one of her hands with his own, a loving gesture from a son, I thought. I wished that I had a parent to whom I felt so close. But his father frowned, and Mrs. Ferguson withdrew her hand.

"Pa," Ker said, "what is it that you want me to do?"

"Pack up your horse, come home, and forget this sinful business of racing. We raised you right . . . and we expect you to honor that upbringing. We've got a ranch to run."

Ker took a deep breath. "I do honor it," he said, "and I'm grateful for the upbringing I've had. But I can't come

67

home. I don't think racing is sinful . . . and Pride is going to win. I know he is."

Conviction gave his voice strength, and I wanted to cheer. Didn't they realize that their upbringing had made Ker the kind, wonderful man that he was — the man who would take in a homeless family for the night, the man who determined to fight when his horse was doped, the man who would keep a stable boy who turned out to be a girl? I had to bite my tongue to keep from exploding with all the impassioned thoughts that crossed my mind . . . and nearly my tongue.

"We need you on the ranch," Mr. Ferguson said. "You could put that horse to meaningful work."

I almost gulped at the idea of Pride, that sleekest of horses, tearing himself up chasing after cattle through mesquite and catclaw.

When Ker said simply, "Pride isn't a stock horse. He's a racehorse," his father stood to leave, and his mother followed suit as though on a puppet string. I noticed that they left the check for Ker.

"Son, we love you . . . but we can't countenance such behavior from our family."

Ker looked startled. "Does that mean I'm not to come home when the season is over?"

"You'll have to figure that for yourself," the father said, patting his son's arm as though in affection — a mixture of messages that I could not figure out.

Mrs. Ferguson managed a quick, "I'm glad to have known you" in my direction and an anguished look at her son before she followed her husband out of the room.

Why, I wanted to shout, don't you hug each other?

Ker, who had been standing, sunk back in his chair and ordered coffee, at which he stared silently for so long that I felt like a speck on the wall. I tried to be silent as long as he wanted to contemplate, but it struck me that I should be getting back to Pride.

"Ker? I'll just go on to the stables . . ."

"What? Oh, Callie," he said, sounding surprised to find me there. "Yes, do go on. I . . . I'm sorry about this, but it was a help to have you here. You deflected some of the anger, believe it or not."

As I left, I saw him put his head in his arms on the table, and I worried that he might be weeping.

Ker had still not appeared when I locked Pride up for the night and went home, thinking dark thoughts about families. Ker had loving parents — to an extent. It was as if they couldn't love him totally, unless he met their rigid standards.

And me? I had a father somewhere, so lacking in love that he never called, never wrote, probably didn't know if I was alive or dead, hale and hearty, or an invalid. Maybe he trusted Aunt Edna that much, but still . . .


Aunt Edna was at her ironing board when I reached home, even though it was well past dusk.

"Aunt Edna, give up for the day," I said, forcing brightness into my tone. "You'll overtire yourself."

"I am tired," she admitted, making her way slowly to her favorite easy chair — the only one in our house.

I made her some of her pale, diluted tea and sat myself down on the stool next to her chair.

"You hang up the faille dress?" she asked.

"Yes," I said with a smile, "and I didn't spill anything on it. Aunt Edna, you'd think I was five years old!"

"Well . . . you just got some growing up still to do," she said, but her voice was fond, almost like I remembered from childhood. Probably, it was just tired, but I chose to hear affection in it.

I drew a deep breath, knowing that I would probably blast the fragile moment to smithereens. "Aunt Edna, tell me about my father. Where is he?"

She was startled and a trifle angry, and her hand moved nervously on the arm of the chair, but she answered with a short, "I have no idea."

"California?"

"Why do you think that?" she asked.

"I don't know. Just a hunch. He used to call me California — remember? I thought that probably meant he was intrigued by it."

"So is everyone else these days," she said bitterly.

I told her about Jimmy Don Russell and his family, though I had to disguise Ker as "one of the horse owners." Still, I stressed how compassionate he was, how poor the Russells were, and how the whole thing made me appreciate our home.

"A big rich horse owner took them in?" she asked curiously. Obviously such generosity did not fit into her rigid picture of horseracing and racehorse owners and — dreaded thought! — gamblers.

"Yes, he did," I said, wanting badly to tell her what a wonderful person Ker was, even to tell her about what a pain Benjie was, and how much I liked Pride. The whole story was close to tumbling from my lips when, instead, I said, "You've never told me why my father left. Just that he had to pull himself together . . . and that's not reason enough for your anger."

She stared hard at me, the fingers doing their nervous dance on the chair. "He . . . he lost . . . the money." She spoke tightly, as if controlling herself only by sheer will power.

"What money?" I asked curiously.

"There was a small inheritance . . . from your grandfather, our father. It . . . it would have raised you nicely. But Bobby lost it." She seemed to relax some in the telling, as though she were releasing emotions long held in check.

"Did he gamble on horses?" I asked, thinking surely that was the reason behind her fervent hatred of the racetrack.

"Of course not. He bought a horse . . . spent all that money on a horse, and then lost it."

"But there were no racetracks," I said, puzzled, "and how could he lose? Just because you lose a bet, you don't lose your horse."

"Men used to race any flat place they could find and they'd bet among themselves. That's how that Colonel

70

Waggoner got started, I've always heard — racing horses on the banks of the Red River against other ranchers. Good enough for them — they can afford it. Your father couldn't."

"What happened?" I prodded gently.

"There were men — con men — who would come around with a nag, a horse that looked like it couldn't go three feet without collapsing, and they'd want to race. Your horse for theirs. If you won, you got this nag, and sometimes they'd add a few dollars. If they won, they got your horse. And, of course, they wanted to race your father's horse, because it was a magnificent animal, big and strong and beautiful. He called it Bonnie Prince Charlie."

"Like the song," I said without thinking, pleased that I knew the connection.

"Like the Scottish hero," Aunt Edna said sharply. "Anyway, he lost the horse. They had two horses that looked alike . . . or were painted to look alike . . . and the day of the race they didn't run the old broken down one. They ran a horse faster than the devil itself . . . and they had little tricks to cheat. They made false starts, until Bonnie Prince Charlie was a bundle of nerves."

"You were there, weren't you?" I asked.

"Yes," she said grimly, "Charlie and I were there. So were you, but you were too young to remember. There were words, afterward . . . and your father left."

"Why didn't he take me?"

"He couldn't . . . and I wouldn't have let him. Any man who'd race a horse that valuable in an offhand bet like that . . ." Her voice trailed off in bitterness again.

"It was a good horse?" I asked, wondering how big the inheritance had been.

"Very good," she said firmly. Then, her voice faltering, Aunt Edna looked at me and said, "It's time I told you more. Go in my room. Under the bed, there's a scrapbook. I . . . I've kept it hidden."

Heart pounding, I went into the bedroom and got down on all fours to peer under her bed. Trust Aunt

71

Edna! Not a speck of dust. But there, pushed well against the wall under the head of the bed, was a leather-bound scrapbook, with the single word "Shaw" inscribed on the cover in gold leaf. And there was not a speck of dust on the book either. Aunt Edna had been taking care of it, maybe even looking at it from time to time, though it beat me how she could get it out from under the bed!

Carefully I carried the book to her and laid it in her lap, and then, with me perched on the stool next to her, she began to turn the pages and open up a whole new world to me.

"This is your Grandfather Shaw . . . he raised fine racing horses in Scotland, raced them in England." And there was a man mounted on a beautiful sleek horse that would have been right at home at Arlington Downs. I couldn't see much about the man, except that he had a beard and a cap of some kind. Because he was mounted, I couldn't tell if he was short or tall, but he looked strong.

Aunt Edna's voice began strong and clear, but wavered as she turned the pages."And this is your father . . . on his first horse." It was a Shetland pony, and he looked to be about three. From there I traced my father's life: jumping at sixteen, racing as an amateur at eighteen, a professional jockey at twenty, married at twenty-one to the mother I'd never known, a willowy beautiful woman who was looking adoringly at her husband . . . and then the scrapbook stopped abruptly.

"What happened?" I asked, wanting to cry out for more. Why had my father left a good career as a jockey to come to the United States?

"The stables burned," Aunt Edna said, her words coming tight and clipped. "Killed all the horses but four . . . and killed your grandfather. We hadn't a thing left, and none of us could bear to stay there. We sold the horses and came to Texas with the money. There was some left . . . that I argued should be for you. Your father said it would be, he'd just use it for that horse first. I cursed him for a fool, and he said he'd never darken my

72

door again. I've taken those words back in my mind a thousand times, but he'll never know."

There was one subject she had skirted around. "My mother?" I asked.

"She died before this happened, thank the Lord. It would've broken her heart. She was frail, and after we got here, she just wasted away, died before you were a year old."

It was a sad story, but almost like one that belonged to someone else, because I could not remember this frail mother of mine, and she was out of my life. My father, on the other hand, still seemed a possibility to me, and I burned to know more about him. "Do you suppose he's still around horses . . . maybe a trainer or something?"

"I suspect so. Bobby never could be away from them for long. And, yes, Callie, I suspect he went to California . . . but I don't know."

"Will he come back?"

She lowered her head into her hands, and I could barely hear her reply. "I reckon not till I'm dead," she murmured. "He loved you . . . almost as much as I do . . . but he is a stubborn, proud man." Aunt Edna burst into great uncontrollable sobs. She had released a flood that had been pent up for years.

I moved to put my arms around her and held her while she cried, great tears running down my cheeks for the father I didn't have, the dream I'd just lost. And I decided right then and there that I'd have to find my father. How to go about it puzzled me some, but find him I would.

Aunt Edna and I sat, silent and barely moving, until well after dark. Her sobs had turned into an occasional muffled cry, but she clutched my hand as though holding on for dear life. I was perfectly willing to sit with her, while my mind dwelt on California and faraway racetracks.

# Chapter 6

# *No Devil Involved*

Frankie Gambrell's father shot himself in the head that night. The tragedy had a lot of ramifications, all of them bad and not the least of them the fact that Aunt Edna found out the truth about what I'd been doing. But it was twenty-four hours before I knew about any of this. I had gone on to work in the morning, going through my usual routine of changing in the shed. I just didn't know it was the last time I'd have to do that.

I hadn't slept well, my troubled dreams full of an angry man on horseback, who repeatedly threatened, "I'll never come back, *never*." In my dream, Aunt Edna stood in the door of our house and held out her arms, pleadingly, and the man just turned and rode away. Not the vision I wanted of my father — and yet, Aunt Edna had said he was stubborn and proud.

As I headed for the stables, my steps slow from weariness, I half wondered if I'd have a job after this morning. Would Ker cave in to his family's wishes and take Pride home? To be disowned by your family was a terrible thing, beyond my imagination. Ker had a family, but they couldn't agree about horses. My father and I would feel the same about horses, but I couldn't find him to tell him that. The world, I thought, was badly out of kilter.

Ker wasn't there for morning exercises, an unusual absence which made me worry all the more. But Pride and I managed to get around the track the required number of times without serious trouble, though I did almost ride right in front of Benjie and Golly Gee. By now, most of the other boys accepted me, with only some slight jabbing comments. This morning, it was Benjie who asked, rather shortly, "Can't you keep your mind on what you're doing?"

"Sorry," I called, wishing I could tell him about Ker and his parents and my family scrapbook and all the things that kept me thinking about everything except where Pride was headed.

At the water fountain, Benjie was a little more curious, but not much. "You all right?" he asked. "You look awful."

"Thanks a lot," I said wryly, pulling at my hair and wishing I'd stopped to look in the mirror. No doubt I'd have seen dark circles beneath my eyes and a face too pale for the lovely day it was.

"Callie?" He was sincere now, and if he asked me once more, nicely, what was the matter, I might give over to tears right there.

"It's nothing," I said, my voice the one that was short and impatient now.

He shrugged. "Have it your own way," and he was gone with his bucket of water.

"Wait!" I wanted to shout, but didn't.

As I curried Pride and mucked out the stall, I kept one ear cocked for Ker. It was midmorning before he arrived, but then he came sauntering along the path, jaunty as ever, whistling "Loch Lomond."

I stood and looked at him in amazement for a minute, and then sang the familiar words, against the background of his whistling,

"Oh! Ye'll take the high road,
and I'll take the low road,

75

and I'll be in Scotland afore ye,
But me and my true love will never meet again,
On the bonnie, bonnie banks of Loch Lomond."

We finished to our own laughter, and I knew that Ker would not be leaving Arlington Downs.

"Sorry I missed the exercises," he said. "Had a bit of business to tend to. It go all right?"

"Except that she rode right in front of me," said Benjie, coming up behind us.

"That again?" Ker asked lightly, and then looked at me. "You look tired this morning, Callie."

"So I'm not the only one," Benjie said.

"I . . . I was worried about you, Ker," I said.

"No need to worry about me," he said, his tone still light. "I'm a survivor."

"But your parents . . ."

"They went home," he said with finality, then with mock sternness to Benjie, who stood staring at both of us, "Hadn't you best get back to your horse?"

"Yes, sir." Benjie was gone before he could ask any more questions, and I was grateful.

I carried the problem of my father around with me all day, uncertain what to do or where to begin, and went home not feeling much better than I had when I'd started the long day. But when I got home, I forgot all about my father for a while.

Aunt Edna had left me a note, instructing me to come to the Gambrells' house. "There's been a tragedy," she had hurriedly written.

Curiosity mixed with dread sent me to the Gambrells' in a hurry, but as I approached, I slowed my steps. Men and women, most in their Sunday clothes, stood in clusters on the small stoop, on the lawn, at the curb. Three or fours cars were parked in front of the small house where, normally, there was no car. Frankie's father had never been able to afford one.

Their looks were solemn as they parted to let me pass through, and though I recognized this one and that, no one spoke. Some men nodded, but the women just looked solemn. A shiver of gratitude went through me that I knew this mourning was not for Aunt Edna. She had, after all, left me the note.

More people clustered inside the small living room. I stood in the doorway for a moment, taking in the scene. Frankie's mother sat on the couch, now and then blotting her eyes or blowing her nose. Aunt Edna sat beside her, leaning toward the weeping woman as though, somehow, she could help by mere closeness. When she saw me, she patted Mrs. Gambrell briefly and made her painful way toward me, but not before Frankie emerged from the kitchen to give me a hateful look that almost shouted, "See what you've done?"

"Aunt Edna?" I asked softly.

"In here," she said, taking my hand and dragging me into a bedroom, closing the door behind us. "Ben Gambrell shot himself in the head last night."

A thousand thoughts went through my mind, none of them helpful and some of them not repeatable. I saw Frankie's anger and her mother's anguish and Aunt Edna's concern. I didn't need to ask why he shot himself.

"He left a note," Aunt Edna said, and then, obviously having memorized it, recited, "'The horse races caused this. The wages of sin are death. May God have mercy on my soul, and watch over my family' . . . . I told you the devil would be amongst us."

"Yes, ma'am," I said, staring at the floor. "What can I do to help?"

The answer came so swift and sharp that I was unprepared for it. "Quit that job of yours at that place!"

"Aunt Edna, I just serve food to people . . . ." Somehow the lie didn't come off my tongue so glibly this time.

And Aunt Edna knew it. "Don't lie to me," she said sharply. "Frankie told me what you do . . . getting a horse ready to race and cheat some poor soul out of hard-earned money." Her eyes were angrier than I'd ever seen them, her face red with indignation.

I sighed. It would do me no good to explain to her

that no one cheated people of their money . . . the man who bets is responsible for himself. Frankie hadn't wanted to understand that, and neither would Aunt Edna. Nor would she want to hear that I was fortunate to have work, that I'd brought home a healthy amount of pay already and expected more. Ker had paid me twenty dollars the first week, nearly three times what I'd earned from Mrs. Langdon.

"What can I do for Frankie or her mother?" I asked, fighting for patience.

"Nothing," she said, her anger turning to sadness. "Why, Callie, why did you lie to me?"

"Because I wanted the job . . . and I knew you'd be unhappy . . . and, Aunt Edna, this isn't the time to talk about it." Just twenty-four hours before, we'd cried together over my father, and now we were at odds again. I bit my lip to keep back a fresh crop of tears.

Aunt Edna put her arms around me. "We'll work through this, Callie. You'll have to quit the job, but we can talk about that tomorrow. Now, you best go home. I . . . I wanted you to know what had happened when I told you to come here, but I don't think you should stay."

"Should I speak to Mrs. Gambrell?" I hoped not, for I had no idea what to say.

"No. She wouldn't know."

We left the bedroom, and I edged across a corner of the living room to the door, thankful now that no one spoke to me. But I counted my blessings too soon. Frankie stood on the stoop outside the door.

"Now you know," she said, "what I tried to tell you."

"Frankie," I said, looking at her pale face, her wide, tearless eyes, "I'm sorry about your father."

"It's too late," she said, raising her voice so that those around us turned to look. "You're part of it, part of that place that killed my father."

"Frankie . . ."

"The Lord will punish you, Callie Shaw, you mark my words."

Her angry voice followed me as I ran down the walk

and away from the house. I was sure if I turned around every eye would be fixed angrily on me.

As I walked home, Aunt Edna's words sank in. "You'll have to quit the job," she'd said. I began to organize speeches to Ker in my mind.

"Ker, my friend's father shot himself after he lost all their money betting on the races. So I have to quit my job."

In spite of my distress and the sadness of the event, I nearly laughed aloud as that speech went through my mind. Suddenly, I could see Ker's incredulous face before me — and he would be right. It made no sense for me to quit my job because of Frankie's father. Frankie and Aunt Edna might not understand, but Ker and I knew that the betting wasn't at the heart of racing, and that we weren't responsible for what Ben Gambrell did any more than we were responsible for the Edgertons winning enough to save their farm.

I waited in the dark for Aunt Edna but fell asleep before someone in a car brought her home at nearly midnight. The motor woke me and I sat up in her overstuffed chair, where I'd been dreaming of a laughing face that was, I thought, my father. And I couldn't figure out why he was laughing, but then his face blurred and Ker was talking seriously to me.

"Callie! You're still up?" Aunt Edna looked exhausted.

"We have to talk, Aunt Edna." I got up to let her sit in her chair, but she simply shook her head.

"Not tonight. I'm too tired."

She was still asleep when I went to work in the morning.

For most of my fourteen years life had gone along pretty routinely. Aunt Edna and I were, to tell the truth, in a rut, even when Uncle Charlie was alive. They worked — he at the store and she at home — and I went to school when I was younger. Uncle Charlie's death brought the only change in that routine. Pretty soon we settled into another one, where Aunt Edna ironed, and I worked at Mrs. Langdon's. Mornings, we ate silently without much conversation; evenings, we were both tired and went to bed early. Life had stretched out before me with the same alarming monotony Frankie had once talked of. Maybe that was why I so often dreamed of a dashing, handsome father who would rescue me.

But in the two weeks since I'd gone to work for Ker, things had happened with dizzying haste: Pride's win and then his loss with the suspicion that he had been drugged, the strained and uncomfortable visit with Ker's parents, Aunt Edna's long overdue confession about my father and her suspicion that he is dead, and then Mr. Gambrell's suicide and Aunt Edna's edict that I must leave the race course. Now there was only one more week left in the race season. Surely, I thought, nothing else would happen in that week — but I was to be very wrong.

I walked to work slowly that morning, trying to sort it all out. I had made my decision, of course. I would not leave Ker and Pride — that was simply beyond possibility. But neither would I tell Ker about Aunt Edna. He had enough to worry about. And I hadn't the faintest glimmer of an idea about how to tell Aunt Edna about my decision, how to stick firm in the face of her disapproval.

I would, I decided, talk to Benjie. In spite of our bickering, he had become my confidante, a better friend than Frankie Gambrell had ever been. The small black cloud that hovered over my head lifted slightly with that thought, and I arrived at the stables in fair humor. But I didn't get to talk to Benjie that morning.

Mr. Bertelli had come to watch morning exercises, especially, I decided, to keep an eye on me. He stood at the rail as we filed onto the track, his hands on his hips telegraphing an attitude of belligerence. The scowl on his face reinforced the message of his stance.

Pride was full of spirit yet willing to follow my guidance, and I was flat enjoying myself as we cantered around the track. Lonnie winked once as he went by, and T. Joe glowered like he always did, but it was Benjie I waited for, wanting a chance to tell him I needed to talk. Slowly it began to dawn on me that Golly Gee wasn't running well. He was in fact almost walking around the track, in spite of Benjie's best efforts and the increasingly irate screams from Mr. Bertelli.

"Give 'im the quirt," he yelled, shaking his fist at Benjie as Golly Gee struggled by. "What's the matter with that horse?"

Though we'd only gone once around the track, Benjie pulled Golly Gee off the course and dismounted by Bertelli who would, I thought, explode at any moment.

The rest of us had to complete the exercises. It wasn't our business what was going on with Golly Gee and Benjie, but there wasn't a one of us that didn't cast a furtive glance in their direction as we went by. Curiosity burned hard and hot.

T. Joe managed to ride close enough to me to say, "It's your fault, you know."

"My fault?" I echoed before I remembered that my policy was just to ignore T. Joe.

"Girl in the stables," he said darkly. "It's bad luck. Only thing is, I'm surprised Poco's Sweet Pride seems okay."

Lonnie came up on the other side of me and called across, "Leave off, T. Joe. Her bein' a girl don't have nothin' to do with it."

I flashed Lonnie a grin of thanks and moved ahead of both of them, not wanting to listen to arguing. A remembered bit of knowledge brought itself to the front of my mind, and I could hear Chance saying, "He rode like mush." Was that how Benjie would describe Golly Gee?

"No," he said when I asked him. "He walked like he was asleep, like I couldn't wake him up."

Since morning exercises I had curried Pride, given him oats and alfalfa, and mucked out the stall, all without a glimpse of Benjie. He must, I thought, have been in the stall with Golly Gee — and Mr. Bertelli. Finally, he'd stuck his head in Pride's stall and asked, "Come outside a minute?"

So there we were, sitting on a bale of hay where we could watch both stalls. Suspicion makes you mighty careful.

"Is he all right?" I asked.

"I think he's okay," Benjie said. "I'm goin' to take him out in the field behind the track this afternoon and see what he does. Bertelli had a fit."

"I saw him at the track," I said. "What happened after you stopped?"

"He kept wanting me to get back in there and use the quirt. I couldn't make him understand that the way Golly Gee was, I could beat him bloody and he still wouldn't run any faster. I don't know . . . ." He shook his head in bewilderment. "Sometimes I can't believe the man's a trainer, he acts like he knows next to nothing about horses. Mr. Waggoner knew about it, he'd have him off this track."

"Really?" There was a new idea.

"Sure. He don't cotton to cruelty to horses. In fact, he's mighty particular about it."

"Maybe Bertelli really isn't a trainer," I suggested, my mind whirling in a new direction.

"Ah," Benjie said, "he is. I didn't mean nothin' by that. Bertelli's just . . . well, he's harsh. That's his way — with horses and people."

"He looks *foreign*," I said, emphasizing the word as if it were a crime.

Benjie laughed aloud. "He is. Italian, by way of New York."

"With ties to gangsters," I supplied instantly.

This time he groaned. "Quit, Callie. Your imagination's gone off again. He was a trainer back east — a good one — and something happened. I don't know for sure, but I think . . . well, I heard he lost his wife in a fire or something awful like that. He . . . well, he sure isn't happy here in Texas."

"Probably feels he's gone to the end of the world," I

said helpfully, feeling some slight pity for Bertelli. "Arlington, Texas, must sound like nowhere to someone from New York." Still, I added to myself, now that he's here, he should know the Downs is as good as any New York track. Besides, pity didn't cancel my suspicions.

I took a deep breath. "Benjie, remember the day Pride ran like mush, or that's what Chance said, and everyone thought he was doped?"

He opened his eyes wide. "Sure I remember. You think that's what was wrong with Golly Gee?"

Before I could answer affirmatively, he went on, "Naw. Why would someone dope a horse for morning exercises, when the horse isn't even goin' to run for two days? I think it was one of those disease — what ya' call 'em? — viruses. Think it came and went, just like that."

Ker was his eternally cheerful self that morning, whistling "When You and I Were Young, Maggie," as he walked along the row of stalls. "Here," he said, waving a piece of paper in the air. "Got a postal card from Jimmy Don . . . they got as far as Tucumcari, New Mexico, and that truck blew out on them, this time for good."

My mind pictured that pitiful family, stuck in a town that sounded like the end of nowhere to me, worse than Texas must have sounded to Bertelli. "I suppose you're going to go get them," I said, half joking.

"Don't need to," Ker answered. "Jimmy Don found work at a grocery store. Just happened to be in the right place at the right time. See, Callie? Everything works to some good — we just don't always recognize it for a while."

Thinking of Frankie Gambrell and Aunt Edna and the way Golly Gee ran that morning, I was hard put to see much good in the events of the last few days. But if Ker wanted to believe that, more power to him.

He sat on a bale of hay and watched me curry Pride. "He's to run the last day of the season," Ker said suddenly. "I forgot to tell you, but I was able to get that third chance for him. Stewards said they'd never heard of a horse running three times in as many weeks, especially one that had boogered his second race. But I insisted."

"Did you tell them he was doped?"

"No. I can't prove that. But I hinted, and they sure don't want any suspicions raised."

"Golly Gee ran like he was doped this morning," I said, watching his face for a response.

"Now, Callie, you know that's not true. Nobody would dope a horse for the morning exercises. Maybe he's getting colic."

Maybe, I thought for some wild reason, they did it just to upset Bertelli. If so, it had certainly worked. Ker was so idealistic that sometimes I thought he didn't live in the real world. Still, both Benjie and Ker dismissed my notion about doping, so maybe I was overly suspicious.

"Ker," I asked, changing the subject, "what if . . . what if your father never talks to you again, you never hear from him. How will you feel?"

"Awful," he groaned. "Why?"

"Just wondered. Seems to me too bad that you can't mend your fences."

"You been listening to him talk?" he asked with a grin. "'Mend your fences' is one of my father's expressions. I always thought it was cowman talk."

"Don't know about that," I said, "but I know about not being on good terms with your father."

"You and your father don't talk?" he asked. Ker knew I lived with Aunt Edna, but beyond that he really didn't know much about me.

"You might say that," I said. "We've . . . we've not seen each other since I was two or three. I . . . I don't know where he is."

"Callie, I'm sorry," he was by my side in an instant, his arm around my shoulders. "I should have guessed, but . . . gosh, what can I do?"

I laughed shakily. "Find me a jockey in California by the name of Bobby Shaw."

"A jockey? You sure?" Ker's eyes lit up. "We could probably do that, if he's really a jockey."

"*If* he's still alive," I said, "he's around horses somewhere. Aunt Edna thinks he's dead." And darned if I didn't start to cry. In spite of biting my lip and talking stern to myself, tears began to roll down my cheeks.

It was almost more than Ker could stand — he hovered, he patted, he offered his handkerchief, and for a minute there, I thought he was going to cry too. He didn't, but he did take the currycomb out of my hand, throw it in the stall, and lead me over to the hay bale.

"Sit down here and tell me," he said, sounding gentle and concerned, like I always thought a father should sound.

The story came tumbling out, me talking fast as though by hurrying I could get it all out before the tears took over. He listened so attentively — interrupting only to say "Oh, my!" or "Really?" or "Poor Callie" — that I told him every detail of looking through the scrapbook with Aunt Edna and then launched into Frankie Gambrell's father's suicide and Aunt Edna's edict that I quit my job. So much, I thought, for being close-mouthed and not worrying Ker.

He did just what I had envisioned. He laughed, though he sobered instantly and said, "I'm sorry, Callie. This is all so tragic that I guess you have to have some release. But the idea that you can atone for a man's suicide by quitting as my stable boy is . . . well, it makes as much sense as my folks wanting me to quit racing because Pride won."

"I'm not going to quit," I said. "But I am going to find my father."

"Right," Ker replied, now businesslike. "And we'll have to think about the best way to do that. I'll ask around — quietly, of course. And I'll talk to your Aunt Edna." He paused a minute. "In fact, I believe I'll take the two of you to dinner tonight."

"Aunt Edna may still be at the Gambrells'," I said, not sure about this plan.

"Then I'll go to the Gambrells'," he answered confidently, which brought a shocked, "No!" from me.

But that's what Ker Ferguson did, went with me to the Gambrells', though I insisted all the way that he turn around. Instead, he followed me up to the door, introduced himself to Aunt Edna in whispers, and then made straight for Mrs. Gambrell, who sat on the couch in the same place she had the previous night.

Before either Aunt Edna or I could say "Stop!" Ker was on one knee in front of her, taking her hand in his, and talking earnestly to her. Mrs. Gambrell raised her sunken head just a little to look at him. Although I thought she would fling him away in anger, she listened intently, and then she began to nod her head in agreement. Finally, while Aunt Edna and I stood collectively holding our breath, they both stood up, and Mrs. Gambrell gave Ker a hug.

Wiping her eyes with the ever-present tissue, she said "God bless you" loudly enough that I could hear it across the room.

"And you," Ker replied. And then he was standing between Aunt Edna and me, saying, "Ladies, I'm taking you to the cafeteria."

Frankie Gambrell stood in the arch between the dining room and the living room, giving me a look that mixed hatred and curiosity. But when she saw me looking at her, she hurried to her mother's side.

We had dinner at the cafeteria, the first time Aunt Edna had eaten outside her own home in over a year. She chose chicken-fried steak — something we never made at home — and turnip greens, while I fought to keep from pointing out that we had those all the time and why didn't she order something else. Ker followed her lead and had chicken-fried steak and greens, but I stubbornly chose roast chicken and mashed potatoes. For dessert, Aunt Edna had a cherry cobbler with whipped cream and ate every bite of it, exclaiming with each mouthful over how sinful it was.

"What did you say to Mrs. Gambrell?" I finally asked Ker.

Aunt Edna looked sharply at me, but I could tell she was as curious as I was.

"I told her gambling was a terrible thing," he said,

and before I could protest, he went on, "and I meant it. It is a terrible thing — I agree with my father. Only thing is, it's like a lot of other things — it's only terrible if you can't control it. Mr. Gambrell couldn't control it."

"If there weren't horse racing, there wouldn't be gambling," Aunt Edna said primly.

"Yes, ma'am, there would," Ker said, giving her his most charming look. "Men have been gambling on everything from cockfights to the weather for as long as we can remember. It's just with horse racing, it's a little more organized . . . and, actually, it's safer for the gambler. There are rules, and as much as possible, we make sure nobody cheats with the horses."

My heart sank, thinking about Pride running like mush and Golly Gee stumbling around the track that very morning.

But Ker went on with all sincerity. "It's a terrible, terrible tragedy about Mr. Gambrell . . . but it isn't horse racing's fault. If he couldn't gamble there, he'd have found some other way."

"Horse racing," Aunt Edna said in measured tones, "brings the devil to walk amongst us. Calpurnia must not continue to work for you . . . and the devil."

Ker looked so astounded I would have laughed if I hadn't been so upset. He had, as they say, been throwing his words to the wind. He looked helplessly at me.

"Aunt Edna," I said, "don't call me Calpurnia. You know I hate it."

She sputtered, but I went on before she could say more, "I am going to work for Ker. We need the money, but it's more than that. I love being around the horses. I love Ker's horse, and I have a special . . . well, a special something with him. We talk to each other. There's no devil involved." I crossed my fingers under the table at this white lie — somewhere, there was a devil involved. We just didn't know who. But we could guess why.

Ker left soon after that, throwing me a look that I took as approval for my stand with Aunt Edna. Maybe it was surprise . . . and a little alarm.

# Chapter 7

# The Colonel's Deal

"**W**hy?" I wailed to Ker, sobbing as he tried to put comforting arms around me. "Why would anyone kill Golly Gee?"

"We don't know that anyone killed him," Ker said in his calmest voice. "Benjie simply found him dead in the stall. You've got to remember that."

I remembered all right — but I remembered that Pride had been spooked in morning exercises once and another day had run like mush, and there was no explanation for either thing. Golly Gee had acted peculiar, to put it mildly, just the day before, and now was dead.

That morning, when I arrived at the track, all the stable boys stood in a solemn knot outside Golly Gee's stall. Occasionally they looked around, as though expecting someone, and before I could ask what was going on, the track veterinarian arrived, carrying his black bag and looking very solemn.

"Lonnie?" I asked, sidling up to him. "What's wrong?"

"Golly Gee's dead," he said through clenched teeth. "Benjie found him just a few minutes ago when he unlocked the stall for the morning."

"Dead?" The word didn't register at first. Not dead, like Mr. Gambrell was dead. Surely not Golly Gee — not Benjie's horse.

"Dead," Lonnie repeated flatly. "Some bugger got to him, I can tell you that."

My head reeled. Two deaths in two days were too much for my mind to comprehend, and I paid no attention to what Lonnie said. It would come back to me later. "Benjie?" I asked.

"In there," Lonnie jerked his head toward the stall. "With Bertelli."

Bertelli! I thought he was the source of all the trouble at the track, was sure of it, and yet here one of his own horses was first doped — or at least I thought so — and then dead. So that made him innocent. But if not Bertelli, who?

Big dumb Walter said, "Must've got the colic overnight. Horses do that, you know." He nodded his head as though to emphasize his wisdom.

"Other things happen too," Lonnie said, and I began to wonder at his grimness. Did Lonnie know something I didn't?

Benjie emerged just then, blinking his eyes when he saw the crowd. Then, wiping quickly at his face with a sleeve, he pushed his way through and started walking toward the track.

"Benjie?" I followed him and called his name softly.

"Dead," he said in tones of disbelief. "Golly Gee is dead."

"I know. Do you know . . . ?" My question trailed off.

"Vet's in there now. But I can't see any sign of anything . . . and he was fine when I left last night."

"Bertelli?" I asked.

Benjie looked sideways at me, his eyes haunted. "Furious. Says it's all my fault. Says I should have slept in the stall."

"Slept in the stall?" I asked with amazement.

"Sure," Benjie said. "Lots of trainers do that, to protect their horses. It should've been Bertelli and not me sleeping in that stall. But I'd've done it, if it would've saved Golly Gee. I'd've put my cot right across that door." He had an odd, faraway look on his face, as though he'd gone someplace that I couldn't follow. "I need to be alone, Callie. I got to think," he said, and he was gone, out to walk around the lonely and empty track.

Morning exercises were late and raggedy. Not one of us could keep a thought on what the horses were doing, and when we cantered past Benjie, my heart near broke for him. He looked up, waved gamely, and then went back to plodding around the track with his head down.

They hauled Golly Gee's body out of the stall while we were at exercises. Benjie had stayed grimly at the rail, never looking toward the stables. I was glad to have missed the sight of the dead horse, and glad that Benjie missed his final exit.

When we got back to the stables after exercises, Bertelli stood forlornly outside the stall. His anger apparently gone, he looked for all the world like a man who had no earthly idea what he was supposed to do next. Once again, I wasn't sure about him. His gray, almost expressionless face was, to me, that of a man who had suffered a great and sudden loss. I remembered Benjie's story about his wife. Bertelli wasn't acting — it was written on his face that he was horrified at what happened to the horse.

And when the man in the limousine drove up, Bertelli was not only horrified, he was nervous. It wasn't Colonel Waggoner's automobile — no, this was a bigger, splashier vehicle, with a uniformed driver in riding pants that made him look like he was in the British army. Formally he held the back door open, and a short squat man in a dark suit emerged. The man held a cigarette in one hand and took an occasional puff from it as he looked around. If Bertelli was nervous, this man was just the opposite. He had that kind of look that said he owned everything in sight. When he saw Bertelli, he nodded ever so slightly, and Bertelli ran toward him.

I longed to be a mouse in the grass and hear that

conversation. Bertelli waved his arms, clasped his hand to his head, and made all kinds of agitated gestures. The other man stood perfectly still, staring straight at Bertelli, hardly even moving his mouth as he talked.

After a few minutes — he hadn't even finished that cigarette — the man in the suit got back into the car, the chaffeur carefully closed the door behind him, and they drove away. Bertelli walked toward the stables, his shoulders slumping.

"Ker," I said, memory flashing back at me, "Lonnie said someone killed Golly Gee."

"Nonsense," Ker said, "you're imagining things."

"No," I said distinctly, "he said, 'Some bugger got to him.'"

"Callie, your Aunt Edna may think the devil is amongst us, but I refuse to believe that there is such a devil at Arlington Downs. A devil who would kill a fine racehorse. And besides, if that were true, the vet would find it out."

"How?" I demanded, anger beginning to replace my unbearable grief. It had struck me, with no small irony, that I grieved a great deal more for Golly Gee than I had Mr. Gambrell, but I figured that Golly Gee was an innocent victim. Mr. Gambrell, in more ways than one, was the architect of his own fate.

"Well . . ." Ker was on shaky ground. His trusting view of the world in general and racing in particular made it hard for him to answer my question with any certainty. "I dont know," he finally said, "he just would."

Lonnie the cynic would know, and I sought him out.

"Air bubble in the veins," he said, his voice still flat and without emotion. "Easy. Can't see a needle stick in a horse."

I was horrified. "Did . . . does . . . did you ever really hear of that happening?"

"Yeah," he said, "but not in Texas ever before. And I

91

ain't the one that told you it might have this time. You remember that. Racing in Texas is different." Lonnie, it appeared, was no spring chicken — he had raced in California and New York — and he went on to tell me hair-raising stories of treachery at the racetrack. Aunt Edna would have said, "I told you so!"

It was only after I walked away that I put two and two together: Lonnie had raced in California! He'd be more likely to know about my father than Chance would. I would ask him, but first I had to find Benjie. I had a more important question for him.

He was once again at the rail, watching as the horses lined up for the first race of the day. I slipped my arm through his, which made him turn slowly toward me.

"You all right?" I asked.

His face was the color of a dirty sheet, and his eyes were rimmed with red, as though, big and old as he was, he'd been crying. "I'm fine," he said, brushing my arm away.

"Benjie, who was the man who came to see Mr. Bertelli this morning?"

"Owns Golly Gee . . . or did."

"He's a gangster, isn't he? From New York? That's why he hired Bertelli." This was not imagination. I'd read enough about the mob in the East to recognize one of their kind who had strayed out west.

Benjie's eyes flew open. "A gangster from New York?" For just a minute, I thought he'd laugh. "He's from Lubbock, Texas . . . lives in Fort Worth now."

I faltered. "But that dark suit . . ."

"Says he wore jeans all his life growing up in ranch country, and now that he's a lawyer, he intends to look like one. He's okay."

"But the way Mr. Bertelli acted . . . like he was threatened or nervous or something?"

"Wouldn't you be if you were in charge of a valuable horse and it died? Burke — that's his name, Robert Burke — is okay, but he's pretty tough. I imagine he gave Bertelli what-for . . . and he should have given it to me."

My mind went in circles, trying to interpret this new information and work it into the scheme I'd constructed in my imagination. I said nothing but stood there while Benjie stared out at the track, only occasionally looking at the horses who danced at the gate.

Finally, the horses were away in the first race — a race in which Treachery, the horse Walter looked after, fell back early and finished last. "A horse to match its stable boy," I said, but my humor fell flat.

Actually, the first three horses in the race ran neck and neck, and it was an exciting race. Benjie never moved a muscle.

"Benjie, will there be an investigation? I mean, if there's a possibility somebody killed Golly Gee . . ."

"It's only a hunch . . . except in your mind it's the truth. Officially he just died. Horses been known to do that before."

"Even when they're favored to win a race the next day?"

He turned a long, dark look on me. "Leave it be, Callie. You'll get into something you shouldn't." And then he turned his back on me again.

"I'll see you around," I said.

"Yeah," he said, without looking at me. "And don't let your imagination go finding any more gangsters."

More than a little indignant, I headed for the stables. As I passed the spot where Colonel Waggoner parked his car, the chaffeur, as haughty as always, called out, "You! You there, the girl!"

I looked around, but there was no one near me, and it was evident that he was talking to me. Still, my voice squeaked when I asked, "Me?"

"You! Colonel Waggoner's been wanting to talk to you."

The door to the car stood open and inside I could see the old man's shrunken figure, a robe over his knees. When I put my head into the door, he said, "You're the girl that masqueraded as a boy." It was a statement of fact, not a question.

93

"Yes, sir."

"Did you bet on Cowpuncher's Boy like I told you?"

The question took my breath away for a minute. "Did you know . . . ?"

"That you were a girl?" He cackled. "Nope, you fooled me. But I heard rumors, put two and two together. Cowpuncher's Boy lost money for both of us." Then the grin left his face. "You know about that horse died this mornin'?"

"Yes, sir." I sat now on the floorboard of the car, literally at his knees.

"Darnedest thing . . . something's going on at my track that I don't like."

I played cautious and said nothing, though I was tempted to blurt out all my suspicions. The name Bertelli would surely have tumbled out in my list of accusations.

"Nothing I can do about it . . . nor no one works for me. Everyone clams up when they see 'em coming." He paused to catch his breath, and I heard a slight rasping as he breathed. "You . . ."

"Me?" My voice really squeaked.

"You can find out what's goin' on. Nobody suspects a girl of havin' brains." He didn't mean it as cruel as it sounded, and I took no offense. "You listen careful, tell me what you find. Pay's a dollar a day till the season closes . . . let's see, seven more days."

"You don't have to pay me." I was uncomfortable about the thought of taking pay from two employers at the same time, though seven dollars was not to be sneezed at. It would have easily bought material for new dresses for me and Aunt Edna both.

A sudden thought struck me. "Colonel Waggoner, did you ever race your horses in California?"

"Nope. But I been to races out there."

"Ever meet a jockey named Bobby Shaw?"

He thought for a minute, while I wondered about old age and memory loss. But then his positive answer washed away my doubts.

"Nope," he said, "never did. Met some owners out

there . . . Gillespie was one, Jim Gillespie. And somebody named Bradshaw . . . but no, nobody just Shaw. Why?"

Why not tell him? "My father is Bobby Shaw. He left for California fifteen years ago, and my aunt . . . well, she thinks he's dead. I . . . I got to know."

"He a jockey?" His voice was alert with interest.

"I don't know," I said miserably, "but he loved horses and was always around them. I just sort of thought . . ."

"I can find out, or at least my people can," he said without a single bit of doubt in his voice. "You find out what's goin' on at my track, and I'll find your pa. Fair's fair."

Reaching out, I put my hand into his for a handshake. It felt dry and crinkly, like parchment paper. "It's a deal."

"Remember," the raspy voice called after me as I turned away, "we only got seven days."

Seven days! In seven days, Pride would run in the final race . . . and in seven days I would be out of a job . . . and maybe never see Benjie and Ker again . . . in seven days I might know where my father was . . . and who killed Golly Gee.

Pride was anxious that day as I curried him, sensing the tension that hung over the stable. So I talked to him about all that had gone on. "Golly Gee's dead," I whispered in that silky ear, "but nothing will happen to you. I'll see to it . . . and Ker will . . . and you'll win next week."

Now I'm not saying that Pride understood every word I said and processed it through his mind, like a human being would have. But in another strange way, he *did* know what I was saying when I told him about Mr. Gambrell or my talk with Mr. Waggoner or even my search for my father. And every few minutes, I repeated, "You're going to be safe, Pride, and you're going to win."

All the while I talked, Pride followed me with his bright, intelligent eyes. He understood me, and he trusted me, in a different way, even, than he trusted Ker.

95

Somehow, the things that I was saying were getting through to him, and I had a special bond with this beautiful horse . . . I really believed that.

"What you have to do, Pride," I concluded, "is win that race. That will show Aunt Edna and everyone . . . there is no devil."

Benjie sat on a bale of hay outside Golly Gee's empty stall.

"Sorry," he muttered, avoiding looking at me.

"Apology accepted," I said. "Bertelli sack you?"

"What's to sack? There's no horse to care for, so there's no job. I can work at the horse farm again. It's not like I won't have a paycheck to take home." He paused. "But I won't get a horse to train this fall, that's for sure."

I stared at him. "What *are* you talking about?"

"Kincheloe — he manages the farm for the Colonel — and he sort of made a deal when he loaned me to Bertelli. Said if I learned a lot from this summer, he'd let me train one of his horses at the farm this fall."

"Benjie! That's wonderful!"

"Not anymore," he said sourly. "Kincheloe will never let me train after this . . . it's like my whole plan's fallen apart. I mean . . . or meant . . . to be a trainer." He looked away, embarrassed, I guess, at how much he'd told me.

"You grow up around horses?" I asked.

His laugh was bitter, and he picked at the hay as he answered. "Hardly. My pa was a farmer, one who never could make a crop, but he was really a good man. Taught me to fish and shoot . . . and to be honest. He died three, four years ago . . . coughed himself to death with consumption. I miss him a lot." He took a deep breath and was silent for a minute.

"Ma," he went on at long last, "she takes in sewing, cooks for a couple of familes. She's really killed herself to see I finished school."

I sat silent, struck by a sense of family intensity I'd

96

never known . . . and envied terribly. "What're you going to do now?" I asked, deliberately changing the subject.

"Don't know. I want to stay around the stables, find out what happened to Golly Gee. Guess I want to clear my name."

"Benjie, nobody suspects you —"

"I suspect myself," he said, "of being careless, not doing all I could. I got to find out."

I debated telling him about Mr. Waggoner's deal with me and decided against it. He'd start in on how it was man's work, not a business for a girl to be messing in. He might even have been right, but I didn't want to hear it right then.

"I'll help," I said, "any way I can." Maybe, I thought, I could talk to the Colonel about Benjie . . . but then I knew Benjie'd hate that.

"Stay out of the way then," he said gruffly. "This isn't something for a girl to mess with, 'specially a girl with an imagination like yours."

Well, at least I'd been right about something.

"Ker doesn't believe me about somebody sleeping in a stall to protect a horse," I said, chewing on a piece of straw. "I . . . I need to convince him."

"Callie," Benjie turned to give me a serious look, "you're not going to sleep in Pride's stall."

"I know, I know. Aunt Edna would have a fit. Besides, you don't know that anything goes on here at night."

"Don't know it doesn't," he said.

I knew then what I would do next.


Aunt Edna had been to Mr. Gambrell's funeral that day. "Fine crowd," she said, taking off her black hat and placing it carefully in the box which had come with its purchase, some twenty years earlier I imagined. "You weren't there."

"No, I wasn't," I said. It seemed of little use to launch

97

into all that had happened that day, all that had erased the funeral clean out of my mind.

"That Ker fellow was there," she said.

"He was?" Amazement echoed in my voice. I'd missed Ker in the afternoon but never thought to ask where he'd been.

"Yes, he was. Sign of respect for the deceased," she said with satisfaction. "He knows where blame lies."

That surely wasn't Ker's feeling at all, but I didn't tell Aunt Edna that. "How're Mrs. Gambrell and Frankie?"

"Seem to be holding up," she said, sighing as though in compassion. There was, I thought, a special bond among the bereaved — it was as though in a perverse way Aunt Edna was glad to have Mrs. Gambrell join her company of the grieving, for she did still grieve for Uncle Charlie.

"You still goin' back to that racetrack?" she asked me over the supper of greens and cornbread I had fixed.

"Yes, ma'am, I am."

She huffed and finally said, "Well, that Ker fellow seems all right. Don't know why he's messed up with all that business, but I guess he'll look after you."

After that we passed the evening in silence, except for the time she said, "That Ker, he married?"

I smothered a grin. "No, Aunt Edna, he's not married. But he's a good fifteen years older than I am, if that's what you mean."

"Take my meaning as you want," she said. "I just asked."

But I knew that she was thinking life would improve a great deal if I were to snare — that was how she would have thought of it — Ker Ferguson. I couldn't explain to her that if anything Ker was more the father I'd never have than the husband I expected to have someday. But not now. Not for a long time.

I pretended great weariness and went off to bed early, only to lie awake for a long two hours listening to Aunt Edna putter in the house. Usually she retired early to ease her aching bones, and I couldn't believe that this night, of all nights, she was up doing this and that, making noises in the kitchen, even talking to herself. If I didn't have my plan, I'd have gone straight to sleep and never heard a thing. But as it was I lay there and listened to every little sound.

Finally, when I thought I'd either burst with anticipation or fall asleep in spite of myself, I heard the springs squeak as she settled on to her bed. A few minutes later I stood by her door and listened to her regular, gentle snoring. Then I was out the door, closing it silently behind me.

It was spooky to walk to the racetrack at night, especially since the night was cloudy and no moonlight guided me as I followed the familiar route. With each step, my anxiety increased — was I foolish to be sneaking back to the track at night? What about Benjie's advice that I'd find something bigger than I could handle? Maybe, I thought, I'd find peaceful, quiet stables and then I could turn around and go home.

My plan was to make my way to a slight rise above the stables where I could sit hidden in the shadows and watch what went on below. I was prepared for long hours of watching a quiet and motionless building, in the off chance that something would happen.

Instead, I came upon bustling activity — at least in one corner. A horse trailer stood outside a stall — wrack my brain as I would, I couldn't remember what horse was assigned to that stall. Even from as far away as I sat I could hear muffled commands and curses, the drumming of hooves on the planking as one horse was unloaded and another loaded on. It was too dark, and I was too far away to identify the horse or figure what was happening. But it was enough to know that horses were being moved in the night . . . and if the move was legitimate, there was no reason to make it in the dead of night.

The hair on the back of my neck rose as I watched. These were men up to no good, and if they discovered me . . . I began to regret my bravado in coming to the stables at night. Still, I told myself, if I sat perfectly still and quiet, and the men down at the stables stayed involved with whatever they were doing, they'd never notice me.

The hand that covered my mouth came out of a silent darkness behind me with such suddenness that I thought my heart would stop beating. Panic rose in my throat, and I struggled against the firm hand that held me.

"Callie, be quiet!"

It was Benjie's voice, reassuring, and yet that hand still held firm over my mouth.

"Will you promise not to scream?"

I nodded my head in agreement, and he released his hold. But his anger was still very much evident.

"I told you *not* to come here at night," he whispered, the whisper in no way hiding the intensity of his anger.

"I . . . well, I had to see for myself. And I did see. What's going on down there?" My voice rose with the question, and his hand was clapped back on my mouth before I could continue.

"Can't you be quiet?"

I nodded, and when he released me again, I whispered a quiet promise not to talk.

"I don't know what's going on," he said, "but somebody's moving horses in the middle of the night, and there's no reason for that. It's no good."

"What are we going to do?" My question came out in a more pitiful tone than I intended, because I was scared . . . for me, for Benjie, and for Pride. "Could those be the people that killed Golly Gee?"

Benjie gave a soft snort. "We don't know that Golly Gee was killed. We just suspect . . . and you keep leaping from suspicion to truth."

"I *know* he was killed," I said with conviction.

"Well, what you'd best do is get Ker to sleep in the stall. Or maybe I will. I'm worried about Pride."

"Why Pride?"

"I bet he'll be the favorite for the final race next week," Benjie said, "and if the pattern follows, that'll put him in danger."

My heart turned over with fear. I would have preferred Pride to be a longshot — and lose the race — than to be in the kind of danger Benjie was talking about.

Below us, the stables were now quiet and empty. The horse trailer had moved out, and the mysterious men with their cursing had moved on. The lights outside each stall shone now on an empty and quiet world. And though we sat for another two hours — with me sometimes dozing in spite of myself and then jerking awake — no one came or went. The horses were quiet, and the world seemed at peace — except that the scene we'd just witnessed destroyed any sense of peace.

"Benjie," I said through a yawn, "what're you going to do tomorrow?"

"Come help you with Pride," he said without hesitation.

I was about to answer indignantly that I didn't need any help with Pride, that I could take care of him myself, when Benjie added, "That'll give me a reason to be around the stables."

"You won't get paid," I said.

"It'll be all right for a few days . . . but not much more," he said ruefully. "Ma really counts on my paycheck."

I couldn't offer to let Ker pay him instead of me — Aunt Edna would have a fit if I stopped bringing money home. And yet I felt guilty, as though I were taking Benjie's job.

"What about what we saw tonight?"

"Don't say anything, even to Ker. Let me think about it," he said with authority.

I bristled. Who did he think he was to make the decisions? "I think I should tell Ker," I countered. "He's got to sleep in that stall!"

"Callie, trust me. Come on, now, I've got to see you home."

There was no arguing with him, though I seethed with frustration as we headed toward my house. "There's no need for you to see me home," I said, indignation creeping into my voice. "I got here by myself, and I can perfectly well get home."

He ignored me and kept walking. When we got to my house, Benjie reached over and gave me a soft punch on

101

the shoulder. "See ya' tomorrow," he said, and went off whistling in the dark.

It was nearly two in the morning when I crawled, still fully dressed, into my bed. My anticipation of the alarm at six made me sleep fitfully.

I greeted the day with puffy eyes and a suspicious spirit. But then I remembered Benjie's punch on the shoulder and I suddenly realized that it was a gesture of affection. All by myself in my bedroom, I blushed a deep red.

# Chapter 8

# Some Answers, But Not All

"K er," I said bluntly, "you've got to start sleeping in the stall with Pride."

"Oh, now, Callie, let's not get that suspicious. I admit some strange things have been going on, but I think they're all coincidence. There's security here, and there's no need for me to sleep in the stall." For all his protestations, Ker had arrived that morning without whistling, a worried look knitting his brows together.

"Then I'll do it."

He was quick to respond. "No, you won't!" After a minute, he asked, cautiously, "What makes you think I need to sleep in the stall?"

I told him what I'd seen the night before. At first, he didn't believe me, but as I went on, giving the details of the horse trailer and the men moving horses in and out, his eyes grew wide, and he began to nod in understanding.

"Is anything different this morning?" he asked.

"Different?" I was puzzled.

Exasperation made him speak sharply. "Do any horses look different?"

"I don't know," I said lamely. "Morning exercises

went as always, but . . . ." I didn't really know what to look for.

"Where's Benjie?" Ker demanded.

Suddenly I realized that it was midmorning and I hadn't seen Benjie yet — strange, to say the least. "I . . . I don't know." And then in a rush I went on, "Benjie would sleep in the stall with Pride," I said. "He's . . . well, he's got no work at the track right now."

Ker flashed me a tight smile. "I guess not, with his horse dead. I . . . I don't really need two stable *boys*" — he emphasized the last word — "but maybe I could put him to work. Tell him I'm looking for him."

It was nearly time for the first race — the race Golly Gee should have won — when Benjie appeared. By then I was worried and angry. "Where have you been?" I demanded.

"Didn't know I had to account to you," he said casually. "Been busy, that's all."

I was so mad at him I thought I'd spit. It wasn't fair for him to confide in me sometimes and other times turn secretive, as though I weren't worth trusting. "Benjie . . ." My threat trailed away because I had no idea what to say next.

"I'll tell you later," he said. "Right now, I need to find Ker."

"He's looking for you too," I said, "but I bet he's gone to the clubhouse to eat."

"Oh, swell." Disappointment settled on his face. "I can't go in there."

"Why not?" I asked. "I did . . . and I'll go again, if you're chicken." I emphasized the last word.

Benjie's look was dark, but he said, "Go on, then. I ain't going in with all those swells, looking like I do."

He had on clean Levis and a denim shirt and only his boots were mucky with stall leavings, so I didn't see that he looked so bad. I probably looked worse, having dressed in a hurry and brushed my hair without ever looking in the mirror. I wondered if the black circles still showed under my eyes.

"Go on, then," he urged.

And so I presented myself at the clubhouse door, where a steward stopped me with a haughty "Yes?"

"Ker Ferguson," I said, "I've got to find him."

The nose was slightly up in the air, and the eyes looked down on me, as though I were a roach on the ground. "Mr. Ferguson is dining with a friend, I believe," he said.

"Fine, I'll find him," and I brushed past the steward to head for the dining room. Behind me I could hear him saying, "You . . . you can't . . ." But I didn't wait to hear what I couldn't. I'd been there before, and I knew where to look for Ker.

He was lunching with the most beautiful woman I'd ever seen. One look at her and I became suddenly self-conscious about my clothes, my messy hair, my plain face, even the freckles that I'd learned to accept. Her hair was not just blonde, it was shining blonde, pulled back smooth against her head and caught in a chignon at the back of her neck. She wore enough makeup that Aunt Edna would have trumpeted about the devil, but it looked right, made her eyes big and dark and questioning and her lips red and pouty. Ker, leaning to light her cigarette, was clearly entranced by this creature.

"Ker?" All the brassiness I'd shown the steward vanished before this sophisticated woman.

"Callie!" His surprise was obvious, though Ker was too sweet a man to ever sound displeased. Still I thought he must have been unhappy to have me barge in at that moment.

"Benjie's looking for you."

He looked blank for a moment. "Benjie?"

I wanted to shout, "Yes, Benjie, you know who he is!" Instead, I said, "Yeah, he says it's important."

"Oh, Benjie," Ker laughed nervously. "Callie, this is Sloan Wilson. Sloan, my . . . ah . . . stable boy, Callie Wilson."

The big dark eyes grew wider. "A stable girl? Oh, Ker, how delicious."

105

While I blushed with indignant anger, Ker flashed me a nervous look. "I'll be along in a minute, Callie. Where is Benjie?"

"He's watching Pride," I said, hoping my meaning about not leaving Pride alone came through. Then, calling up my best manners, I said to the Sloan creature, "It's nice to have met you. Excuse me if I have to run."

Her amused expression followed me out the door.

"A floozy!" I yelled at Benjie. "He's absolutely hooked on a floozy!"

Benjie laughed so hard he almost fell off the bale of straw on which he sat, and I, for one, was so glad to hear him laugh again that I kept on. "He lights her cigarettes, he stares into her eyes! I tell you, Ker is a lost cause, Benjie. He'll be no help at all."

"You're jealous," Benjie hooted, while Pride watched the two of us with wariness. I wished he could join in the conversation, for I thought probably his opinion would be the most sane.

"I am not jealous! I just . . . well, I didn't think Ker was paying attention to how important this is."

Benjie sobered. "I'll pay attention," he said. "If Ker's found himself a lady friend, let's let him enjoy it. You and I can take care of Pride."

And that's exactly what happened.

Benjie never would tell me where he'd been that morning, but when Ker came I listened to their conversation. Benjie had been to see Robert Burke, Golly Gee's owner, because Burke had sent for and tried to hire him as a — well, the only way I could later say it to Benjie was "snoop."

"Investigator!" he retorted.

Whichever, Burke wanted Benjie to stay around the track on the pretense that he was working for Ker and to keep his eyes and ears open, but Burke would pay him and Ker wouldn't have to. Burke, it seemed, was especially distrustful of Bertelli, his own trainer.

"What did you tell him?" I asked.

Benjie looked uncomfortable. "Told him I couldn't do it. Bertelli hired me . . . and it doesn't seem right to spy on him. I don't know, but the whole thing sounded wrong to me."

Another plus, I thought wryly, for intuition. Somehow I was glad Benjie had refused . . . even though I was sure about Bertelli's guilt.

Ker was almost unconcerned about the whole thing and clearly anxious to be away to watch the first race — presumably with Sloan. "I'd pay you to stay in the stall," he said. "I . . . ."

Benjie completed the sentence for him, "You don't want to sleep in the stall, and I will. You don't have to pay me."

"I'll pay you," Ker said firmly, but he looked relieved. When he added, "I do have dinner plans," I almost snickered out loud, biting my tongue to keep from asking, "With Sloan?" What kind of a woman had a first name like that?

Telling us to take care in a kind of offhand manner, Ker went whistling away toward the clubhouse. As far as he knew, his horse was safe, the world was a wonderful place, and all problems were solved.

I didn't feel that way about it at all, and I was glad Ker had left. I had answers to demand from Benjie before I went to see Mr. Waggoner at his car. "Benjie, what happened last night? Did you find out?"

"Nothing," he said. "I've asked around and no horse has been moved. Guess we didn't see what we thought we saw."

"Impossible," I said angrily.

I was still fuming when I sat on the running board of Mr. Waggoner's limousine.

"Whoa," he said, his crackly voice breaking now into a chuckle. "I never could understand a runaway horse. Back up to the starting gate one more time."

107

So I told him about the switch of horses we'd seen during the night, and Benjie's calm dismissal of it, and which owner trained which horse, and Mr. Burke's trying to hire Benjie. "It doesn't sound right to me," I ended.

"Robert Burke's a good man," Mr. Waggoner said, hands moving absently across the robe which covered his knees. "He's on our side. But I don't know 'bout this other business. You keep on, missy." He reached into his pocket, extracted a roll of bills, and pulled one off to hand to me, while I sat gaping. I'd never seen a roll of dollar bills before in my life.

"Thank you," I managed. "Did you find out anything . . . uh, from California . . . ?" I didn't want to be pushy.

"No," he shook his head slightly, "but I put out some inquiries. Takes time, girlie, takes time."

Time, I thought, was what I didn't have, what with the season ending and all.

B enjie was with Pride, but itching to be freed. "I got to watch this race," he said, "you stay here with the horse."

Pride's ears pricked up, and I knew he didn't like being referred to as "the horse."

"But I want to watch too," I complained, just barely keeping my voice below a whine.

"One of us," he answered with great patience, "has to stay here with this horse, and it isn't gonna be me right now. I got to see who wins the race Golly Gee should have won."

My indignation subsided, and I nodded to show him I'd stay. "But come tell me as soon as you can."

He agreed.

All the other stable boys were out at the races . . . except Lonnie, who was apparently doing the same thing I was, for he never went further than three feet from his horse's stall.

"Hey, Lonnie," I called.

108

"Hey, yourself, Callie," he called back, waving a hand but making no effort to move from the bale of hay where he sat, enjoying the October sun. Behind him, Wonder Boy held his head over the bottom of the stall door, nuzzling at the top of Lonnie's head. In an automatic gesture, Lonnie reached behind to rub the horse's muzzle.

I walked the distance between the two stalls — there were maybe ten stalls in between — and sat next to Lonnie.

"I been wanting to ask you something," I said, "something personal."

He looked startled enough to run but managed his usual flip retort. "Just don't call the cops. I'll confess to anything."

"Lonnie, I'm serious . . . when you rode in California, did you ever know a jockey named Bobby Shaw?"

He looked long and hard at me, but his expression was inscrutable. "Bobby Shaw? Why?"

"He's my father . . . or at least, he *was*." And I told him the whole long story.

Lonnie took a piece of straw out of the bale and began to chew on it, his eyes fixed on the rise of ground beyond us where Benjie and I had hidden last night. After a long time — or it seemed long to me — he turned to look at me. "Yeah, Callie, I knew him in California."

A numbness, a kind of feeling of unreality crept over me. Here, for the first time ever, was someone besides Aunt Edna who knew my father . . . and would admit to it. Behind me, vaguely, I heard the roar of the crowd and knew the first race was over.

"Was he . . . did he . . . where?" I didn't even know what I wanted to ask.

"Santa Barbara," Lonnie said slowly. "I rode for him. He wasn't a jockey . . . he was a trainer."

Now a thousand questions rushed into my brain. "When? How long ago?"

"Six years ago," he said, now without hesitation, as though he knew the time span by heart.

"Where is he? How can I find him?" I was ready to rush to the phone right then.

"Don't know, Callie. I . . . uh, I moved on . . . far as I know he could still be working for Nathan Upchurch."

"Nathan Upchurch of Santa Barbara," I repeated. "What stables?"

"Gold Coast Racing Stables," Lonnie said, his voice so flat that it stopped me cold just as I jumped off the bale, ready to run to find a phone, any phone, and call California.

"Lonnie? What is it?"

His look was far away again, as though he saw something I didn't. "Nothin', Callie, nothin' that matters anymore."

Instinct told me that whatever it was had to do with my father and that it did matter, that I couldn't just rush off and call the Gold Coast Racing Stables to ask for Bobby Shaw. I *had* to know! "Lonnie?" I sat back down beside him.

He shook his head. "Weren't nothin', Callie. If I can help you find your pa, that's good. And that's all you need to know about it."

Suddenly I remembered Pride, and though I'd been sitting within yards of his stall, I hadn't really been watching. Without another word to Lonnie, I ran back to the stall. Pride munched contentedly on the oats I'd put out earlier, and turned to stare at me as I burst in.

For no good reason that I understood I threw my arms around Pride's neck and sobbed. I'd found my father — or at least a trail to him. But something, maybe something in Lonnie's expression, warned me I might not want to know what I'd find at the end of that trail.

Benjie Thompson, I thought angrily, you get back here! That race is over!

Benjie came back with the news that Fancy Dan, the new favorite, had won the first race.

For a minute, I forgot about Lonnie and my father and the mysteries. "Favorite?" I echoed. I counted back on my fingers. "Benjie! Of all the races we've been keeping track

110

of — races Pride or Golly Gee rode in — it's always been a longshot that won. How come now it's the favorite?"

He threw me a withering glance. "Favorites usually win," he said. "That's why they're favorites."

"But this horse shouldn't have been . . . Who trained him? Who owns him?"

"Trainer is a guy named Ed Smith . . . seems okay to me, but I don't know much about him. Program says the owner is Judd Kincheloe of Dallas . . . never heard of him. And, for what it matters, Chance rode him today."

The names rattled around in my brain, but I could make no sense of them. The only known factor was the jockey . . . and he wasn't, couldn't have been, part of any plot.

But I had another big thing on my mind, and I didn't want to share the Bobby Shaw problem with Benjie, though it occurred to me that he and I were terrific at keeping secrets from each other and then getting mad about it. "Benjie," I said urgently, "stay with Pride. I got to go somewhere . . ." And I was out the door before he could stop me.

Running, I made my way to the spot where Colonel Waggoner's car was always parked. I was desperate to tell him what Lonnie had revealed about the Gold Coast Racing Stables . . . but the car was gone! I couldn't believe it — the last race of the day not yet run, and the colonel had already left. A tiny twinge of fear went through me. What if something happened to the old man? Not only would I not earn the remaining six dollars he had promised me, but, more important, he couldn't help me find out about the Gold Coast Stables and a trainer named Bobby Shaw. Frustrated, I stamped my foot . . . and bit my lip so hard it almost bled.

"Benjie," I said, back at Pride's stall, "are you going to sleep with Pride tonight?"

"Yeah, but I'd sure like some supper." His sidelong look was a not-so-subtle hint.

"Did Ker say anything about bringing you food?" I

111

couldn't believe that Ker would just walk away, but that's apparently what he did.

"No. Said he'd see me in the morning," Benjie growled.

"All right," I said. "I'll bring you supper." It meant a long walk home, then back here and home again. Not that I had anything else to do with my Saturday night or that I would have left Benjie without food. But still — Ker was the one with a car and the one whose horse was involved. I knew where he was, though — or at least who he was with.

A norther blew through just as I started home, one of those pale autumn northers that doesn't turn the air blue and doesn't really make it that much colder but still brings enough of a hint of fall that you feel a sudden chill. I shivered as I walked home, and wondered what I'd say to Aunt Edna.

"Callie? You're home early, child." She looked up from her ironing board.

"Got to go back, Aunt Edna. Just need to get something."

"What?"

Her voice became suspicious, demanding. Yet if I told her I was taking some of our food, scarce as it was, to feed one of the stable boys, I knew she'd turn to anger. Fortunately, my answer of "Oh, just some clothes," seemed to satisfy her, and she made no move to leave her ironing board.

"How's your arthritis today?" I called from the kitchen, while I opened a cupboard door with the stealth of a safecracker.

"Pretty bad," she said. "Must be the norther that came through. I could feel it in my bones all day."

"I'm sorry," I called, silently spreading peanut butter on three slices of bread, topping it with jelly, and finishing the sandwiches off with three more slices of bread. I wondered if Aunt Edna counted our bread . . . or measured the peanut butter. Still, it was the most filling, most healthy, easily transported food that I could think of.

"All this worry," she said, almost as though in a

monologue. "The Gambrells are a burden . . . don't know how they're going to make out."

"Frankie's got a good job," I replied, silently wrapping the sandwiches in wax paper and reaching for one of the two remaining apples in the bowl. Benjie would just have to do with water to drink.

Aunt Edna made a noise that sounded like *"tsk, tsk,"* followed by, "Frankie! What can she do to support a family? The girl's dancing to be off on her own. I thank the Lord, Callie, that you're as responsible as you are — even if you do work in *that* place." Her sigh of despair was clearly audible in the kitchen.

A tight band fastened itself around my chest, threatening to cut off my breath. "Thank you, Aunt Edna," I managed to say. "I . . . well, I'm grateful for all you've done for me."

Her voice softened. "I know you are, child, and I'm thankful you're as good as you are. I suppose that Ker fellow looks after you, in the midst of all that . . ." Her voice trailed away. The evil at Arlington Downs was too great for words.

What, I wondered, would she say if I told her Ker was suddenly spending all his time and attention on a slick blonde who smoked cigarettes? I made a fast turn from the kitchen to my bedroom, the bag of sandwiches hidden behind me. In a minute, I emerged, carrying the bag.

"Need to take a shirt to one of the stable boys," I said, my guilt made all the more intense by the lack of logic in what I said. Why would I need to take a shirt to a stable boy? Aunt Edna never suspected a thing. I would have felt a little less guilty if she hadn't been so trusting.

"Well, don't be late," she said. "I've got a tin of ham for supper. Mrs. Anderson brought it when she picked up her husband's shirts."

Ham loaf! For someone who'd eaten in the clubhouse at Arlington Downs, ham loaf didn't have much appeal. "Sure, Aunt Edna, I'll be back as soon as I can."

"Peanut butter!" Benjie was indignant. "Dry peanut butter at that, without a thing to wash it down."

"Come on, Benjie, I couldn't tell my aunt I was bringing you food, and besides, it's filling. You won't be hungry."

"I won't be able to pry my tongue loose from the roof of my mouth," he said. But then he softened. "Thanks, Callie. I know you did the best you could. And I know your aunt will probably be furious if she finds out."

"She won't," I said with false security. "Wonder where Ker is and what he's eating."

"Champagne and steak," Benjie said without hesitation, "and we don't have to wonder who he's sharing it with."

I felt oddly jealous and was in a foul mood when I left Benjie, though I have to say that he wasn't much happier. "Take care of Pride," I said unnecessarily.

"Sure," he answered flippantly, "what else am I here for? See you Monday."

It hadn't really dawned on me that the next day was Sunday, and I had no reason to be at the track. Ker usually took care of Pride on Sundays, and now with Benjie there, I was doubly useless. It gave me an odd feeling — I wasn't sure I could handle a whole day away from the track and all the intrigue that it involved. In my mind, I envisioned a day spent gnashing my teeth and wondering about doped horses, lost races, and missing trainers named Bobby Shaw.


Sunday turned out to be different from my bleak expectations, though not much better. I knew how it would go from the minute Aunt Edna wakened me with, "I thought we had two apples. Did you eat one?"

"Yes, ma'am," I faltered. "I just thought an apple sounded so good last night . . ."

"That's fine, child, I just wondered what happened to it."

114

Guilt bit into me again.

"I've promised Mrs. Gambrell we'd be over today. Goin' to take some food. How about you make that ham loaf you was too tired to make last night?"

"Of course, Aunt Edna." I dragged myself out of bed and before I was really awake began mixing canned ham, bread crumbs, pickle relish, and mustard into a loaf — not a wonderful thing to do first thing in the morning.

Nothing would do but that I accompany Aunt Edna to the Gambrell house, though I tried to plead tiredness, the need to wash clothes, and, finally, Frankie's anger at me. "It's your Christian duty," Aunt Edna said firmly, and I knew there was nothing for it but to put on my decent Sunday dress — not my best, but a decent one — and head off down the street, with Aunt Edna walking grimly beside me. I got to carry the ham loaf.

We expected to find hardship and despair. Instead, we found plenty and a serene, if not happy, atmosphere. The dining room table was laden with food — a ham, a pot of pinto beans, biscuits with gravy to spoon over them, and a cobbler for dessert. Our ham loaf looked pretty pitiful.

"What . . . where . . . ?" Aunt Edna couldn't quite bring herself to ask, and yet she was dying to know where all the food came from.

"Mr. Ferguson brought all this food over last night," Mrs. Gambrell said. "You know, he is such a *fine* man. I'm afraid in my grief, I would have misjudged him . . . but he is not at all what I expected from someone at that track. He's honest and caring and . . . well, I don't know where we'd be without him. He's going to speak to someone in Dallas about work for Frankie. And he says I'm not to worry, he'll find me some work too."

My mouth hung open until I finally managed to echo, "Ker came here last night?" When the nod was yes, I asked, "Was he alone?"

"No, a Miss Wilson was with him. Beautiful woman, truly beautiful. My, but I was impressed . . . and she helped me put the food up and all. Come, do eat some."

115

Frankie still didn't speak to me, but she had gone from looking daggers to a kind of glum silence. Occasionally I caught her glancing at me, but her anger lacked force. Mrs. Gambrell kept patting my knee and telling me how grateful she was that I'd brought Ker into their lives.

Ker Ferguson, I thought, was a real puzzle. Just when I thought he'd flipped into love and forgotten everything else in the world, he does something totally unselfish like this.

Jimmy Don Russell and his family floated into my memory, and then suddenly the thought hit me that maybe I too was one of Ker's charity cases. Maybe he didn't really need me at the stable at all but was just giving me work because he thought I was pitiful. All of a sudden, I was angry at Ker all over again, but for a new and different reason.

And Sloan Wilson? Where did she fit?

When Aunt Edna and I were back home in the early afternoon, I fully intended to sneak off to the track. But I lay down to close my eyes for just a moment — and slept a sound and dreamless sleep for four hours. I spent the evening pacing, envisioning a thousand catastrophes at the stables — danger to Pride, a threat to Benjie, even an ominous black cloud hanging over Ker.

Monday morning I ran all the way to the stables.

# Chapter 9

# The Investigation Stops

To my absolute disgust, it had been a deadly quiet weekend. I expected Benjie to be waiting anxiously for me, full of sinister news to report. Instead, I found him still asleep on the cot which he and Ker had placed so that it blocked the door to the stall.

"Bertelli told me to do that," Ker had said wisely. "Nobody can get in without waking you up . . . or tripping over you."

"Is Bertelli going to sleep in a stall?" Benjie had asked in disgust.

Ker had looked thoughtful. "Don't know. I didn't think to ask him."

By Monday morning, Benjie had had his fill of sleeping on a cot, with hay all around him and a horse looming over him. I couldn't care less that he was dirty, itchy and angry at the world. I wanted to hear that strange men had been prowling the stalls, that horses had been moved, even that someone had tried to enter Pride's stall.

"No," he said, stretching and rubbing his eyes. "You could give a person time to get out of bed."

"A person," I said haughtily, "doesn't have to sleep the day away. It's time for morning exercises."

He grunted. "You bring me anything to eat?"

"Biscuits and a cold piece of ham loaf," I said. It was the best I could do, but I wasn't about to be apologetic about it. Ker probably wouldn't think to bring anything for his newly hired night guard.

Benjie slowly brought himself to a standing position and bent one leg and then the other, as though working out the stiffness. Then, without another word to me, he grabbed his tin cup and headed off to the water spigot.

I moved the cot so that I could go to Pride, who nuzzled me in welcome. "You're a lot more glad to see me than he is, aren't you, boy?" I asked, stroking his nose. "And you don't demand so much. I'll get you fed soon as we have morning exercises."

Back with a cup of water, Benjie sat on the cot and ate his cold breakfast.

"You're sure nothing happened?" I asked, still unwilling to believe him.

"So quiet it was almost spooky," he said, and then added quickly, "Not that I was afraid."

Wordlessly I began to saddle Pride.

Disappointed, I remembered that I promised Mr. Waggoner some news by today. I was actually fiddling the day away until time for Mr. Waggoner to be at his customary spot. I had intended to trade information for his help, tell him what Benjie had learned in exchange for asking him to call the Gold Coast Racing Stables. Now I had no card to trade. I'd just have to ask. Meantime, I had to get through the morning — exercises, chores, and Benjie's grumpiness.

Pride was frisky, full of himself, and ready to run at exercises. I had to hold him back, and I did it less by the reins than by whispering in his ear. "You're ready, Pride, but you have to wait. Save your strength for the race on Saturday. Don't let them see how great you are now." A slight twinge of fear shot through me as I said that. If Pride looked too good, he'd be in danger — again. I looked

118

over my shoulder and saw Benjie studying the horses intently. Beside him, Bertelli was in deep conversation with — of all people! — Chance. Ker was nowhere to be seen.

Lost in my ride on Pride and my secret whispered conversations with the horse, I had no more thoughts for Bertelli or Chance as we circled the track. But the minute we were back in the stable, I demanded of Benjie, "What was Chance Donnelly doing at exercises?"

"He's Ker's jockey," Benjie said mildly. "Maybe he wanted to see how Pride looked."

"He told Ker it was stupid to race Pride again. And, besides, he was talking to Bertelli." I couldn't let go of my suspicion of Bertelli, though I'd long ago erased Chance from my list of evildoers, even if he was the most arrogant man I'd ever met.

"Chance rides for Bertelli too," Benjie said wearily. "You're barking up the wrong tree, Callie. Besides, I did make some notes this weekend — while I was waiting for nothing to happen," he added bitterly.

"Notes?" Are we in school? I wondered. I wanted action, not words on a piece of paper.

"Notes," he said firmly. "I tried to make a pattern out of winners and losers, longshots and favorites, even who owned what horse and what jockey rode." He waved several sheets of paper in front of me. "Remember when you said that horse Chance rode shouldn't have won because he was a favorite? Made me think . . ."

"And?" I asked breathlessly, sure that he had found the key to what was going on at the track.

"And nothing," he said. "It doesn't make sense. That was the only favorite that won all last week. And . . . we don't know about Golly Gee."

"But Golly Gee and Pride both were favorites . . . and one got doped and the other's dead," I persisted. "The key is there somehow."

"What about the favorite that won?"

"I don't know," I said unhappily. "I can't figure it out. How about jockeys? What has Chance ridden?"

Benjie almost grinned. "It's no wonder Chance is in a

foul mood. That was the only winner he's ridden since Pride won as a longshot. And there's no pattern to other jockeys . . . Kingsley rode a winner, so did Herb Patterson, Jimmy Johnson, a whole string of them. After all, there's been a string of races every day all week. But no one jockey wins all the time . . . and no one owner."

Benjie went home to change clothes while I curried Pride and put out his oats and hay and did all my morning chores. Ker appeared whistling but not looking quite as cheerful as usual.

"How were exercises?" he asked.

"Fine. Ker . . . I thought . . . well, I thought you'd want to see how Pride was running, what with the big race almost here and all."

He winced. "I did . . . I mean, I intended to be here, but . . . I overslept. Sloan and I went to Dallas for dinner last night, and I guess the time just got away from us . . ."

He put his head in his hands, though I couldn't tell whether from embarrassment or a headache. I suspected both. According to Aunt Edna, the demon rum was only slightly less evil than the devil brought to us by gambling. And I suspected that Ker had been indulging in that lesser demon.

After a bit, he raised his head and asked, "Benjie? Anything happen this weekend?"

"Nothing," I said almost bitterly. "Benjie's gone home to change."

Ker looked plainly relieved. "See? I told you this was all unnecessary." He glanced at the cot which I had by now folded and put out of the way in a corner of the stall.

"Ker Ferguson," I said, daring to be bold, "if you want to take that chance with this horse, tell Benjie to go on home at night." I was afraid I'd offended him, but still I felt strong enough about it that I had to speak my mind. To my relief, he grinned — the first such expression from him that morning.

"No," he said, "'cause if I did you'd just sneak over here and spend the night, and I don't want that to happen."

After a bit Ker left, saying he was meeting Sloan in the clubhouse, and quick as he was gone, Chance appeared. I had the definite sense that Chance was waiting for Ker to leave before he made his presence known.

When he came into the stall, I simply looked at him, waiting for him to speak. Chance Donnelly had been rude enough to me more than once, and I saw no reason to speak first.

"You rode him well this morning," he said, his voice just a shade less hostile than usual. "Better than I thought you could do."

"Thanks."

"Horse looks good," he said. "I might've been hasty in refusing to ride him Saturday . . ."

For my money, I'd have told him to forget it, but I knew Ker wanted him to ride, so I said nothing.

"I . . . I can't afford to ride many more losers," he said, almost confidentially. "Word gets around, and I won't get any rides if I don't win some of the time."

I thought he sounded petulant, but I said nothing.

"You think he'll win?" he finally asked, and I nearly fell over to think that Chance Donnelly was asking my opinion.

"Yes," I said, "I think he'll win."

"I watched . . . you have a special feel for him. Doesn't happen often, never to jockeys 'cause we ride so many horses. But sometimes between a man and a horse . . . uh, or a girl and a horse . . . something develops and there's no explaining it. You have that with Pride."

I blushed a little, which he took for agreement.

"I'll ride or not, depending on what he looks like Friday," Chance said, the old arrogance creeping in, "but I'll be listening to what you say . . . and I'll be at morning exercises."

With that, he was gone, and I was left to think how far I'd come as a stable boy in two weeks. Chance Donnelly was asking my opinion!

121

By the time Benjie made it back, people were streaming into the track for the afternoon races, and I was dancing a jig of impatience. From the hill near the stable, I watched the parking lot fill while I kept one eye on Pride's stall. I was looking for that particular black automobile. Three times I saw vehicles that could have been Colonel Waggoner, but from the distance I couldn't be sure.

Benjie came strolling back just minutes before the first race and then he only came to tell me he was going to watch the race, so I should stay with Pride.

"No you're not!" I said and ran off before he could stop me. I looked just once over my shoulder and saw him standing in front of the gates, hands on his hips, his mouth sending out words — but I was too far away to hear them.

Running almost blindly I bumped into three people — one a nicely dressed woman who assumed all the blame and kept saying "Oh, I'm so sorry" as I stooped to pick up her purse, one a man in a suit who said, "I say now!" indignantly and sounded like he was from England, and the third, Sloan Wilson, who reacted angrily until she looked at me.

"Aren't you Ker's . . . uh . . . stable boy?"

"Yes," I said, shifting from one foot to the other. "Sorry, I was in a hurry."

"Oh, no harm done." Her light laugh had a false ring to it.

For just a second I stopped to look straight at her and decided there was something in Sloan Wilson's eyes I didn't like. I could just imagine Benjie saying, "Oh, come on, Callie!" But it was true. Maybe I would tell Benjie . . . and maybe I wouldn't.

What I did was to tell Mr. Waggoner. In fact, I blurted out every suspicion I had, none of it backed by fact.

When I arrived breathless at his car, I would have yanked open the back door — closed, apparently, against the slight wind of the day — and thrown myself at his feet if the chauffeur hadn't reach out and stopped me. His

122

iron hand clutching my arm, I almost hung suspended in space.

"He's expecting me!" I said indignantly.

The cool answer was, "I'll tell him you're here."

He did that and then ceremoniously held the door open for me with a bow low enough to be mockery.

Throwing him a dirty look, I said hello to the old man. Was it my imagination or did he look more frail every time I saw him, as though he were fading, day by day?

His voice, though, was still sharp. "You've been running, girlie. That mean you got something important to tell?"

"Yes," I said, still panting from my run. "The Gold Coast Racing Stables in California . . . Santa Barbara . . . owned by a man named Nathan Upchurch. Do you know him?"

The answer was too quick. "Nope. Never heard of him. Why?"

"My father trained for him," I said. "Lonnie — one of the stable boys here — knew him. But he wouldn't talk about it. Said it was a long time ago and not something he wanted to remember." With a jolt, I realized Lonnie had said he'd ridden for my father. Did that mean he used to be a jockey and was now a stable boy? That would be a real come down, if so. And if my father had anything to do with that, it was no wonder Lonnie was bitter about him.

He shook his head. "Don't sound good, girlie. I'll find out. Now what have you found for me?"

"Nothing," I said miserably. "Benjie stayed with Pride all weekend and said it was so quiet it was boring."

"You trust this Benjie person?"

I flared in anger. "Of course! Don't even suggest —"

His cackle of a laugh interrupted me. "Okay, okay. I just asked. He your boyfriend?"

I was equally indignant this time. "Of course not!" Then I added, "He works at your horse farm. Mr. Kyle . . . K . . . ."

"Kincheloe," the Colonel supplied.

"That's it. He loaned Benjie to Bertelli this summer."

I hesitated ever so slightly, then plunged on. "Benjie wants to be a trainer someday. He'd be good."

"That so?" the Colonel asked with a marked lack of interest, and I decided I could say no more about Benjie's thwarted plans.

We talked a bit more and my indignation subsided, replaced by the urge to talk. I almost blabbered, telling Colonel Waggoner all of my suspicions about Bertelli, how I felt about Chance Donnelly, even Ker's new infatuation with Sloan Wilson.

"How," I asked, "can he get so goofy over her in two days?"

The old man smiled, as though remembering. "It happens," he said. "But Sloan . . . ain't that a funny name for a woman? Seems to me I've heard 'bout someone named that before. Just can't recall."

"I don't like her," I said flatly, shifting to ease my legs which were cramping. I'd been crouched in the door too long.

"You're probably jealous," he said, and then laughed because he knew he'd made me mad again. "Now go on with you. I want to listen to the races. You come back tomorrow."

Dismissed, I wandered to the railing to watch the races. Lonnie stood next to me.

"Chance's ridin' for Bertelli," he said. "Horse called Lone Star. Longshot."

Absently I listened to him without hearing. "I'm . . . I'm trying to find out about the Gold Coast Stables," I told him.

He looked sharply at me. "How?"

"Just asking," I said vaguely.

"If I were you," he said, "I'd let it lie."

The same advice I was always getting from Benjie. "I can't," I said.

Lonnie, who never showed any emotion, suddenly grabbed my arm — tightly — and shouted, "Look, Callie, look!"

Lone Star was a full length ahead of the second

horse and closing in on the finish. A roar went up from the crowd when he crossed, much of it a roar of disappointment from those who'd bet on the favorite.

Lonnie had calmed down again now and all he said, in a low mutter, was "Elephant juice."

Elephant juice? I'd heard that before, but where? It dawned on me — Chance had accused me of giving Pride elephant juice the day he won. I still didn't know what it was, but I did know it somehow hyped a horse up so that it ran incredibly fast, even if injured. Or that is what Ker had told me.

"Was it really elephant juice?" I asked Lonnie, but he just shrugged.

We stayed there while Chance met Bertelli and the owner in the winner's circle. To my surprise, the owner was Robert Burke — the man who had hired Benjie, though I thought by now he must be disappointed in his investment. But I recognized him because of his dark suit that looked like he was going to a funeral. Finally, the ceremony over, a stable boy — someone I didn't recognize — walked the horse away.

"Lonnie, that horse is limping!"

Lonnie looked. "Sure is. Might've pulled a tendon. If it was elephant juice, horse would run like hell anyway. Seen good horses ruined that way."

"Ruined?"

"They run on an injury . . . makes it permanent."

By unspoken agreement, we turned back to the stables.

Benjie was pacing, no less angry than when I'd left him a couple of hours earlier. "Enjoy the races?" he asked sarcastically.

When I told him about Lone Star and Lonnie's theories about elephant juice, he forgot his anger and listened intently. "Burke owns Lone Star," he said.

This new bit of fact sounded ominous, but I couldn't figure out why. I rolled it around in my mind and tried to remember Benjie's sheets of papers with all the races and horses, but still no pattern emerged. Burke just hadn't been a part of anything, except for owning Golly Gee.

"I talked to Bertelli this morning," Benjie said slowly.

"He still think it was all your fault?"

He shook his head slowly. "He's gotten over that. But Callie, he's scared . . . scared of something I don't understand. He won't talk about it, but I can . . . well, I can just see it."

I went home gratefully that night, glad to be away from a puzzle so tangled it made my brain ache, glad even to be away from Benjie, who was cross about spending the night, not being able to figure out what was going on himself, and feeling that he owed Mr. Burke some kind of a solution.

"Bring me some breakfast," he commanded as I left.

"Sure," I said.

I dawdled on the way home, though it was cool and the wind still blew enough to make me pull my woolen outer shirt tight around me. It hadn't been three weeks since I walked home from the track for the first time, dressed in a sticky and uncomfortable dress on a hot afternoon. Now here I was dressed like a boy in work clothes and chilly enough to wish I was home in bed. But the weather wasn't all that had changed . . . I had changed, and I knew it.

I'd fallen in love with a horse, and I'd gotten myself in the midst of a mystery that could turn really ugly — Benjie had warned me sternly, "Whoever killed Golly Gee, if they did, and doped Pride, if they did, isn't playing some kind of light game!" — and I was on the verge of finding out something about my father, something I probably didn't want to know.

Since Aunt Edna had told me the story of our family, I'd constructed a thousand lives for my father, imagining him as a jockey, a trainer, a stable owner, rich man, poor man, beggerman, thief. But in all of them, I could find no reason that he had never written me, never shown any interest in me. It was fine to say he was stubborn. I'd inherited some of that myself. But this was stubborn beyond understanding. I was afraid I would find someone that I didn't like at the other end of the search — and that meant giving up a dream that had carried me through seventeen years.

"Aunt Edna? I'm home." The house was dark and quiet enough to alarm me. Usually I found her bent over her ironing board, no matter what time I came home.

"In here," came a soft call from the direction of her bedroom.

Aunt Edna lay on her bed, fully dressed, an afghan pulled over her, a wet towel on her forehead. "I . . . my head aches fiercely," she said, "I thought I'd just lie down for a bit. I'll be better shortly."

I felt her forehead, but it was cool from the wet towel. Her face didn't feel hot, and I remembered that when I was a child she always felt my back, not my forehead, to see if I was feverish. Her back was cool.

"When did this start?" I asked.

"About an hour ago," she murmured. "Go on and fix your supper. I . . . I can't talk."

Panic rose in me. Nothing could happen to Aunt Edna! Where would I be without her? Even angry as I got about her belief in the devil and crossways as we'd been about the racetrack, she was all the family I had. Especially since I was about to lose the dream of my father. Forcing myself to sound calm, I said, "I'll be in the kitchen if you need me."

She didn't reply, and I left, pulling the door almost but not quite closed behind me. In the kitchen, I puttered, not feeling like supper yet thinking I should eat. I also needed to put something up for Benjie's breakfast. As I poured flour for biscuits into a bowl, I heard Aunt Edna moan. Brushing the flour from my hands, and leaving a trail across the living room, I hurried to her room.

"Aunt Edna?"

Instead of answering me, she moaned again, louder,

and then, piercingly, cried out, "I can't stand it!" Within seconds she was limp, unconscious. My instinct was to shake her awake, an instinct I fortunately suppressed. With shaking hands, I dialed the number of old Doctor Barnes, who'd taken care of me as a child — neither Aunt Edna nor I had been near a doctor in years. As soon as I identified myself, in a voice as shaky as my hands, he asked, "What's the matter, child?" and I described Aunt Edna's behavior. "She's . . . she's still asleep," I said.

"Breathing regular?" he asked efficiently.

"I . . . I think so."

"I'll be right there," he said.

Then I called Ker and blurted out my story. Like the doctor, he said he'd be right there, and he actually arrived first — but he had Sloan with him.

"Callie, dear," she said, "we're so worried! What can I do?"

I wanted to suggest she wait in the car. But even in my fog I knew I couldn't be rude, so I just shook my head. There wasn't time for anything else to be said before Doctor Barnes arrived, carrying his little black bag. With barely a nod, he disappeared into Aunt Edna's bedroom, and I stood, waiting, just outside the door. Ker stood beside me, a comforting arm on my shoulder, and Sloan sat on the couch, watching us in a way that would have made me uncomfortable if I'd paid any attention to it.

"Sorry," I whispered to Ker, "I must have interrupted your dinner." Later it would dawn on me that Ker and Sloan had progressed from fancy dinners in Dallas to intimate dinners at home.

"I'm glad you called," he said, "and Sloan doesn't mind . . . do you?"

She shook her head quickly.

The doctor emerged almost too soon. I guess I wanted him to be puzzled about what was wrong. Instead, he seemed to know instantly. "She's had a stroke," he said. "No telling at this point how bad it is, but I think she's best off in my clinic."

"Clinic!" I echoed. "Doctor Barnes, there's no money

. . . can't I take care of her at home?" Even as I said that I realized that becoming a nurse would mean abandoning Pride before his big race, and letting Ker down, and . . . not seeing Benjie, cross as he was.

"The money's no problem, Doctor," Ker said quickly. "Do whatever is best for her . . . I'll take care of it."

"Ker . . ."

"Hush, Callie, let's just get her to the hospital."

Between them, Ker and Dr. Barnes carried Aunt Edna to the doctor's station wagon and laid her gently on the back seat. I crouched beside her on the drive to the hospital, holding her hand and whispering to her, though she still hadn't come back to consciousness. Ker and Sloan followed in Ker's truck and stayed with me at the hospital until Aunt Edna was settled.

Dr. Barnes' clinic had ten beds and, this night, five patients and one nurse. Aunt Edna made six, and I thought I could pay more attention to her than this poor nurse. But then, the nurse knew what to look for and I didn't. I waited impatiently in the small, shabby lobby until they had dressed Aunt Edna in a gown and put her in bed. Then I spent the rest of the night sitting by her bed, holding her hand, listening as she occasionally moaned and turned in her sleep. By morning, I was exhausted, and Dr. Barnes sent me home to sleep.

"The worst of it is over," he said. "Now we'll just have to wait and see how bad the damage was."

I went home and slept until midafternoon, waking with a start and almost calling, aloud, "Pride!" Then I relaxed — Benjie would take care of Pride.

I went back to the hospital and, because of Aunt Edna, spent the entire day away from the racetrack. It was late evening before it came to me that I'd also spent the day away from Colonel Waggoner and whatever news he had to report.

Aunt Edna was almost herself, at least in spirit, when I got back to the hospital. She was alert and angry because she could not make her left arm do what she wanted it to.

"We're lucky that her speech is not affected," the doctor told me. "She can probably learn to reuse that arm, but it will take time. But she'd better stay here a day or two more, just for me to watch her."

Aunt Edna greeted this news angrily. "Got no business being here. Calpurnia, you tell him I'm going home. Person can't sleep in this noisy place."

Maybe I thought we'd have been better off if her speech had been temporarily affected. "Aunt Edna, you slept soundly all night. I was here. And you can't go home . . . I have to go back to the stables, and I can't take care of you."

That was a white lie. Ker would have paid me even if I never showed up at the stables again, but I couldn't do that. I had to know what happened. I had to be there for Pride to run in Saturday's race — and I had to find out about Bobby Shaw and the Gold Coast Stables. When I was panicky about Aunt Edna, I'd forgotten all about the stables and my father, but now that I wasn't worried about her — or at least, as worried — it all came crashing back to me.

In the end, she agreed to stay at the clinic, and I went home late that night, promising to return the next night.

"You're going to the racetrack tomorrow?" she asked indignantly.

"Yes, ma'am, I am. I have to." Oh, Aunt Edna, I begged silently, please understand!

"It's the devil's own work," she muttered and turned her back on me.

# Chapter 10

# Long Distance Call

Pride greeted me with a soft whinny of joy the next morning, but Benjie's noise was all anger, which made Pride look sideways at him. "Where've you been?" he demanded. "It's not just that I nearly starved to death till Lonnie got here and fetched me a sausage, it's —"

"Benjie!" I interrupted. "Didn't Ker tell you?"

"Ker?" he asked. "I haven't seen Ker in two days. Where *were* you?" His anger was turning to curiosity.

"You haven't seen Ker?" I couldn't believe what I was hearing. How could Ker go a whole day without coming near Pride? A whole day when he knew I wouldn't be there?

"Is there an echo in this stall?" Benjie asked. "No, I haven't seen Ker, and I haven't seen you. I even rode Pride in morning exercises yesterday . . . and was fixing to ride him today."

"You can," I said quickly, "but here's a piece of cornbread I brought you." Actually the cornbread was three days old and probably stale, but I had nothing else to offer him. I'd wrapped a warm moist paper towel around it, hoping to soften it on the way to the stable.

He took a bite and then, swallowing hard, said, "Never mind, I'll stick to day-old sausage. Here, I'll saddle Pride while you tell me where you've been."

Standing in front of Pride, I stroked his nose, while I told Benjie about Aunt Edna's stroke, my long night in the hospital, Ker's help, and how yesterday had evaporated into sleep.

"Gosh," he said sincerely, "I'm sorry I jumped you. I just couldn't believe . . . don't you need to be with her?" He saddled Pride while we talked.

"Nothing I can do for her," I said, my fingers crossed just in case it was a white lie, "and I need to be here . . . for Pride . . . and, well, to see what's goin' on." It bothered me some not to tell Benjie that the Colonel was calling California on my behalf . . . but then I could already hear Benjie's disapproval. So I kept that to myself.

"Nothing's goin' on," he said bitterly. "I'm beginning to think we've imagined all the troubles that have happened. Here, I'll give you a leg up." He cupped his hands and waited for me to mount.

"Won't you ride him?" I asked.

Benjie shook his head. "Pride does a whole lot better when you're on him. He and I were almost as bad yesterday as you were the first day you rode him in exercises."

I couldn't keep from grinning. "Surely not that bad . . ."

"Yeah," Benjie said, "that bad."

The sky had closed in with low-hung clouds by the time we went for exercises. There was a wet cold in the air — not the pleasant crisp bite of the norther a few days earlier but the kind of cold that crept into your bones and spirit. It would rain, probably only a mist that wasn't enough to do the land any good but more than enough to make everyone miserable. Still, these days we were grateful for anything wet, and I knew better than to complain.

I gave myself a strong lecture on not letting my mood affect Pride, and it must have worked, for he behaved beautifully during exercises, circling the track with an energy and vigor that put the other horses to shame, his head held high, his movements sure as his long legs ate up the track. I was simply along for the ride — and to whisper in his ear, telling him how wonderful he was. When exercises were over and I gave him a sugar cube, he nuzzled at my chest, telling me he had missed me and was glad I was back.

But Ker never showed up, not even when we were back in the warm comfort of the stall, out of the wet and cold.

"Benjie? I'm worried about Ker."

Now that I was back to do the work, Benjie lounged on the hay and watched me curry Pride. "Worry's not the point," he said. "He's just keepin' busy with that Sloan woman. Trouble is, he shouldn't be ignoring his horse that way. Makes me mad."

It made me mad too. But how could I be angry with Ker, who had appeared so promptly when I needed help with Aunt Edna? "I can't believe he's . . . well, that his head's that much turned by her," I said.

Benjie laughed at me. "Maybe it'll happen to you someday, and you'll understand."

Benjie's tone implied that it had happened to him before, a worldliness that made me both curious and a little jealous. I blushed and turned toward Pride, whose look was one of contrasting innocence, telling me he knew I'd never desert him.

By the time Ker appeared, it was almost post time and the hour when Colonel Waggoner usually looked for me. I was ill disposed to talk to Ker, no matter how grateful I was to him or angry at him. He came along the stalls with that distinctive limping swagger of his, whistling "When You and I Were Young, Maggie," as though he had not a care in the world. Benjie, fortunately, was gone to jaw with the other boys, though I'd warned him to be back an hour before the first race, and he'd challenged me with a rude, "Who says?"

"Ker," I demanded, "where have you been for two days?"

"Busy," he answered vaguely. "I knew you'd take care of things . . . you or Benjie."

"I wasn't even here yesterday . . . and you knew that!" My anger showed in my voice and probably in the red that crept up my neck and face.

"Callie," he asked patiently, "are you scolding me?"

I drew a deep breath. "Yeah, Ker, I think I am. Your horse is going to run a major race in four days, and you're too busy romancing a . . . well, you know, romancing, to come to the stables and see to his training."

Ker gave me a long look, all the laughter gone from his eyes. "I seem to remember that I'm the boss and you're the employee, and that I have a great deal of confidence in you . . . maybe too much . . . but I assumed you would know that what I was doing was important and that I trusted you with Pride."

This wasn't the Ker who was daft about Sloan speaking, the one who drank himself into a hangover and ignored his horse for two days. Instead, this was a deadly serious Ker, the one who'd taken a feast to the Gambrells and shown up at the clinic to see about Aunt Edna. Before I could even think about reconciling the contradictions in this man who stood before me, Pride kicked a hind foot at the stall wall, as though expressing, for me, the anger that I kept hidden.

"How's your aunt?" Ker asked, returning to his usual manner.

"She was cross and crotchety last night, so I figure she's doing all right. I'll go by tonight," I said sullenly.

Benjie still hadn't appeared, and I figured I'd get my revenge. "Ker, will you stay with Pride? I . . . I want to watch the first race."

Ker eyed me suspiciously. "You're going to watch in this weather?" A drizzle had begun to fall, just enough rain to make it miserable . . . and to make the track slippery.

"Uh, yeah, I've got a favorite in the first race."

He no more believed me than did Pride, whose eyes — I swear — were laughing. Before Ker could disagree, I was out the door, calling over my shoulder, "I'll be back. Don't leave him alone."

Ker shrugged resignedly and disappeared back into the stall.

As I hurried the length of the stables, grateful for the small overhung roof which at least kept me dry until I reached the parking lot, it suddenly occurred to me that Mr. Waggoner probably wouldn't be there, because of the weather. He might take a chill in the wetness, at his age. But if he wasn't there, how could I wait another day to hear about Bobby Shaw and the Gold Coast Racing Stables?

To my relief he was there. Not only that, the chaffeur was standing in the rain, peering in my direction as I approached the Ford. "Where you been, girl? Colonel Waggoner was looking for you yesterday." His temper apparently was not improved by the weather.

"I . . . I was detained," I said. Darned if I was going to explain myself to this puppet in fancy clothes. "Can I talk to him?"

"I'll see," he said condescendingly, and then opened the back door of the car and leaned in to speak to the Colonel in whispers.

"The Colonel," he announced, "will see you."

You'd have thought I was in a fancy drawing room being presented to the king of England, rather than waiting to talk to a plain old Texas cattleman who'd been waiting for me for two days. "Thanks," I murmured, hoping I looked appropriately grateful — or sarcastic.

"Girlie," the Colonel said as I seated myself next to him on the seat. It was too cold for me to sit on the floorboard and leave the car door open to blow in on him. "Where've you been? I looked for you yesterday."

I told him about Aunt Edna and he was nicely sympathetic, until he asked, "How old is she?"

"I don't know . . . maybe sixty or so."

His laugh was almost a cackle. "I'm eighty-seven," he said. "Just proves what hard work and right living do for the constitution."

135

Aunt Edna, I thought, would never believe that. While pushing him toward an early grave for his association with the sinful business of racing, she'd have been claiming that she was the one who had lived right and worked hard. But I wasn't there to talk about longevity and right living.

"Did you . . . did you find out anything?" I asked, my heart pounding against my ribs with the question.

"Your pa — if Bobby Shaw is your pa — is the head trainer at the Gold Coast Stables, man in his forties now. So what are you going to do about it?"

I was dumbfounded. I'd supposed that the Colonel — or whoever did his investigating — would have told Bobby Shaw the whole story. "You didn't tell him?"

He laughed. "I didn't have anything to do with it. One of my people called out there, talked to the owner in my name, found out what you wanted to know, and reported back to me. Far as I know, nobody has told Bobby Shaw anything . . . at least, that was my instructions."

I stared at him, impressed again by his craftiness. I hadn't thought through what would happen if someone found Bobby Shaw, or what he should be told. "Well, I guess I want you to tell him . . ."

His sharp voice interrupted me. "Wait a minute, missie. I found him for you. Beyond that, my services aren't required. You want to tell him something, you tell him yourself." He paused and looked at me and then said, kindly, "I'll even pay for the phone call. You can call from the office here at the track, on my word."

My heart, beating wildly one minute, now threatened to freeze and never beat again. What would I say to my father after thirteen long years?

I was back in Pride's stall before the first race began, much to Ker's confused pleasure. "You changed your mind?" he asked, echoing my weak excuse for being back so soon.

"Yeah," I said, biting my lower lip hard to keep back the tears which threatened to come at any moment.

Ker was so wrapped up in his own world — or in

136

Sloan — that he never noticed my unhappiness. "I'll be in the clubhouse," he said.

As soon as I was sure he was far enough away not to hear me, I buried my head in Pride's neck and gave in to sobs of despair. I should have been dancing with happiness that my father had been found. Instead, a strange feeling of dread had come over me, and I had no idea of what to do next.

By the time Benjie came back to the stall, my eyes were puffy and red, but I knew what I was going to do.

"You okay?" he asked, real concern written on his face.

"Sure," I muttered. "Must've gotten something in my eye. I . . . I gotta go see about my aunt now. You take care of him the rest of the day?"

Benjie looked startled. He obviously hadn't counted on being confined to the stall this early in the day. "Ker coming back?"

I shrugged. "He's in the clubhouse . . . probably with Sloan. I gotta go," I said, leaving him no choice.

But I didn't head for Aunt Edna and Doctor Barnes' clinic. Instead, I went back to Colonel Waggoner's car, knocking on the window for the chaffeur to let me in. The Colonel still sat in the back, wrapped in his warm robes, the window cracked just enough that he could hear the noise of the racetrack.

"I want to make that phone call," I said.

The old man cackled happily. "Thought you had the stuff in you," he said. Then, calling to the front, "Williams! Take this girl to the office. She needs to make a phone call. Here's the number." He fumbled in a pocket and pulled out a folded scrap of paper, handing it to me. On it was written simply a phone number and the word, "Shaw."

"Thanks," I muttered.

"Let me know what happens," he said, and turned his attention back to the race. The announcer was just posting results from the third race and informing the crowd that neither jockeys nor horses had been hurt in a tangle that had happened on the third turn.

Williams marched ahead of me to the clubhouse, never looking back to see that I was following nor indulging himself in one cordial word. Inside, he turned into the office area, spoke briefly to a woman who sat behind a desk reading a magazine and chewing ferociously on her gum, and left, all still without speaking to me.

"You can use the phone in there," she said, motioning toward an adjoining room with her head. "You know how to make a long distance call?"

I shook my head, almost unable to speak because of the combination of dread and anticipation that had taken over my whole being.

"Just ask the operator," she said, not unkindly but not with a great deal of interest either. She turned her attention back to the magazine she'd been reading when Williams interrupted her.

With shaking hands, I picked up the receiver, dialed "0" and watched the dial spin all the way back, as though I were watching something in slow motion.

"Operator," the disembodied voice said. Then, when I failed to say anything, the voice became sharper, "Operator!"

"I want . . . I want . . . to call California." I wished my heart would stop pounding.

"City and number?" She was still impatient with me.

My voice almost breathless, I told her Santa Barbara and read off the number. "It's the Gold Coast Racing Stables," I added, thinking to myself that I had to make my voice stronger — and myself more confident — before Bobby Shaw came on the line.

When a bored voice answered, "Gold Coast," I took a deep breath, lowered my voice as much as I could, and said "Bobby Shaw, please." Even to my own ears, I sounded less unsure.

"Shaw?" The voice called off in a distance, then speaking into the phone, said, "Just a minute."

"Thanks," I said, still making an effort to speak slowly and confidently.

It must have been five minutes — I worried a great deal about the Colonel's phone bill during that long wait — before a man came on and in a brusque voice said simply, "Shaw."

"Bobby Shaw?" I asked, my voice rising in spite of myself on the end of the question.

"Yeah?" He was curious now.

I took another deep breath. "This is Callie . . . Callie Shaw."

Silence. What if he slammed the phone down, really didn't want to hear from me ever? What if he asked for proof that I was who I said I was? What if . . .

"Callie?" Now his voice had a tremor in it. "Where are you?"

"In Texas," I said, thinking I should add, "Just where you left me." But I didn't. "Aunt Edna's had a stroke," I said. "I thought you should know."

"Is she all right?" He was on firmer ground now, if Aunt Edna was the reason I called. I sensed that if I had simply called to say that I was his daughter, calling after all those years, the conversation would have been impossible. Maybe Aunt Edna's stroke was one of those blessings in disguise she always talked about.

"She's cross," I said, "so I guess she's all right. She's in Doctor Barnes' clinic."

"Okay. I'll call there." Another long pause. "How are you?"

"I'm fine," I said. "And you?"

"Oh, fine, just fine. I keep meanin' to get to Texas . . ."

"Yeah," I said. "It would be nice if you did." There were a lot of things I wanted to tell him, not that I wanted to start in on "Where have you been for thirteen years?" I could tell him that I worked in a stable and all about Pride. But something, maybe his own caution, held me back. "I gotta go," I said. "I'm using someone else's phone."

"Oh, yeah, sure. Thanks for calling."

*Click,* and it was over. After all those years I'd found my father — and he was still a stranger.

139

It didn't help any that I found Ker waiting for me by the magazine-reading secretary. "Callie? I saw you come in here . . ."

"I had to make a phone call. Colonel Waggoner let me use this phone."

Ker's eyes widened. "Colonel Waggoner? Why, Callie, I didn't know you were acquainted." There was laughter in his voice again, this time directed at me. "You continue to suprise me," he said.

"Yeah," I said. "Well, I visit him at his car while he watches the races."

"And this phone call? Anything I should know about?"

I shook my head. "Just telling a relative in Caifiornia about Aunt Edna," I said. Well, that was barely a white lie. I didn't even have to keep my fingers crossed. "I gotta go see her now."

"I'll drive you," Ker said.

"I'll walk. You . . . you have other things to do."

"Sloan will wait for me in the clubhouse," he said. "This is not a debatable matter. In fact, neither is lunch. I bet you haven't eaten."

Sloan was gracious and full of concern for Aunt Edna when Ker brought me to the table they shared. Ker ordered me a chicken sandwich, but I barely ate half of it. He attributed my lack of hunger to concern about Aunt Edna, and I didn't correct him. We left Sloan, still smiling, at the table, and Ker drove me to the clinic.

"Give your aunt my best," he said. "I . . . I don't think I should take the time to come in right now."

Of course not! *Sloan* was waiting for him. "Sure," I said. "Thanks. See you tomorrow."

He nodded and drove away almost before I got the door on the passenger side closed.

Aunt Edna had moved from indignation to self-pity, but in spite of herself, she looked better. Her color was not quite as pale, her eye looked a little stronger. Her left arm, however, still lay useless on the top of the bedcovers.

"I'm a great deal of trouble to you, Callie," she said in a soft voice.

I wasn't fooled by the voice, sure that if she had chosen indignation again, the voice would have been stronger today than yesterday. "It's no trouble, Aunt Edna," I said, crossing the fingers of one hand behind my back. "I'm just glad to see you looking better."

"I don't know what we'll do," she said, her voice almost a whine. "I can't take in ironing this way." She cast a bitter glance at the useless arm.

"Doctor Barnes says you may regain use of it. You'll just have to retrain it."

"He brought me a tennis ball." Indignation crept back into the voice, "As though I needed a toy right now."

"Tennis ball?" I couldn't figure out what she was talking about.

"Says I should practice gripping it with my hand. But I told him my hand won't hold anything. I can't do it." Back to self-pity.

"I don't suppose you can do it in the first five minutes you try," I said, hazarding a guess as to how long she'd worked with the ball. "I expect it will take days and days . . . you'll just have to keep up with it."

A long sigh was my reward for suggesting patience. She turned her head away from me.

"Aunt Edna," I said, going to the other side of the bed and taking hold of her good hand, "why didn't you ever try to find my father?"

Bless Aunt Edna! She left self-pity behind and turned a clear eye on me. "I did," she said, her voice turning firm. "I . . . I got the idea he didn't want to be found."

Didn't want to be found? Why wouldn't he, when he had a daughter that he supposedly cared for? "Why?" I asked.

"Oh," she loosened her good hand from my grip and waved it in the air, "I'd get close to finding him . . . and then the trail would be cold again. I tried off and on for a few years . . . and then, well, I just gave it up. After all, we'd never moved from the spot where he'd left us. He knew where we were, if he wanted to find us."

"Aunt Edna," I took a deep breath, "I talked to my father today."

"You *what?*" She looked so startled that it occurred to me I could give her another stroke, just from the shock of the news.

I waited a minute but all she did was stare intently at me. "I talked to him today," I repeated. "I thought he should know you'd had a stroke."

"And?" Now her voice was penetratingly sharp.

"He said he'd call the clinic to check on you . . . and that he keeps meaning to come to Texas."

A snort was her answer to that, and then she reached that good hand toward me. "Callie, you and I will do fine. We don't need your father." So much for self-pity!

"Sure we will," I said, bending to give her a kiss on the forehead. In that last minute, she'd become the Aunt Edna I remembered from my childhood, the Aunt Edna I wanted back.

I left her to go in search of Doctor Barnes, who told me she was doing fine, showed no signs of another stroke about to happen, and that her recovery would just take time. When I told him about my father and Aunt Edna's reaction to my news, he chuckled and said, "A little healthy anger might be the best thing for her right now. Ah . . . there's something I should add to this."

I looked questioningly at him.

"Your . . . uh, father . . . called this afternoon, apparently right after you called him."

"He did?" I knew he said he'd call, but somehow I didn't think he was concerned enough.

"Yes. We chatted about your aunt. I assured him she was in no danger."

My spirits dropped just a bit. I suppose maybe I'd been hoping that Bobby Shaw would be concerned enough about his sister to finally make the trip to Texas. But if he knew she was all right, he wouldn't think it was necessary. On the other hand, he hadn't thought it was necessary to see his daughter all these long years, so maybe I was foolish to even think he'd appear in Texas.

Doctor Barnes patted my hand sympathetically and went about his business. No doubt he had more serious patients to worry about.

When I went back to the room, Aunt Edna had placed the tennis ball in her left hand again, and I could see her concentrating on it, though as yet there was no movement in the hand.

"I've been thinking," she said. "How long is that awful racing season going to go on?"

"Through Saturday," I answered.

"Then I'll go home Sunday," she said. "And then we'll see where we are, and what we have to do."

Most of me was delighted that she'd turned agreeable and that I could take care of Pride without worrying about Aunt Edna. But money worries made a large gnawing hole in the back of my brain. A week in the clinic! With Ker footing the bill, I supposed it was possible. But it made us heavily indebted to his good nature, and, increasingly, his good nature seemed to come and go, depending on Sloan. I didn't trust her good nature at all. No need to bother Aunt Edna with that right now.

"I really think that's best," I said. "I'll come by every night to check on you, but I'll do whatever Ker needs me to during the day." There! Another slight white lie! I'd take care of Pride, but I would not, I swore, become a whipping boy for Ker when he felt badly and hung his head in his hands, like he did that one morning.

Still, in spite of those nagging worries, I went home and slept the sleep of the righteous, nearly sleeping the clock around. I still woke in time to be at the stable early. I'd get to wake Benjie, I thought smugly as I half-ran the two miles.

Yesterday's rain and chill had vanished — what was it they said about Texas weather? If you don't like it, wait ten minutes and it'll change. It certainly had, for though the air had an early-morning crispness about it, the day promised to be sunny, warm, and perfectly wonderful. It matched my spirits.

143

# Chapter 11

# The Disappearance

The whole world fell apart when I got to the stables.

I couldn't open the stall door. Oh, it unlocked all right, but it wouldn't push open. Something seemed wedged against it from the inside.

"Benjie! Benjie, let me in!" There was no answer, so I tried again . . . still no answer. Then, in desperation, I called, "Pride?" hoping for an answering whinny. There was no sound in response, and my heart fluttered in panic.

"What's up, Callie?" Lonnie asked, strolling casually along the stall doors.

"I can't get in!" I said, my voice rising in desperation.

"Give me the key." Lonnie's bored tone indicated he thought I was falling to pieces over nothing. I'm sure he thought he'd solve my problems with a snap of his fingers — or a twist of the key in the lock.

I handed it to him, even as I wailed, "It's not the lock!"

He found the same thing I had, but he was strong and pushed harder, and pretty soon he had the lower door open enough for him to stick his head in. His words did not reassure me.

"Holy Mother of God!" he exploded.

"Lonnie!" I screamed. "What is it?"

"It's Ker," he said, "and . . . I think he might be . . . dead."

The word was heard but not registered. If it had been, no doubt I'd have fainted right away — and I've always hated fainting women. "Dead?"

"I don't know," he said. Then, with a dexterity that I would have admired mightily under most circumstances, he reached up and around to unlock the top half of the door, swung it open, and then leapt lightly through that opening. Turning to look at me, he got angry for the first time. "Don't just stand there, Callie! Go call somebody!"

I ran, not sure even where I was running or who I was calling. But run I did, screaming hysterically as I went. "Help! Ker's dead, somebody, help!" In no time, not surprisingly, a crowd had begun to gather around me. "Pride's stall," I shouted. "It's Ker!" Having run almost a circle around the stalls, I headed back to Lonnie . . . and whatever was left of Ker.

Lonnie had pulled the cot out of the stall. It was Benjie's cot, with a senseless Ker lying on it, that had been blocking the stall door. From a short distance away, I looked at Ker lying there lifeless, with the stable boys all standing around, and Lonnie bending near him, talking earnestly.

"Ker!" I screamed again.

Lonnie stood up, holding out a hand as though to silence me. "He's not dead . . . quite. But he's sure out like Lottie's eye. I don't know what it is . . ."

Bertelli walked up, looking haunted as he had in the past few days, and said, "I'll go for my truck. Lonnie, you watch him." He half-ran toward the place he always parked his battered truck.

"Pride?" I asked, turning toward Lonnie, my voice still high-pitched and frantic.

Lonnie nodded. "In the stall, calm as can be."

With barely a glance toward Ker, I was into the stall. Pride stood eyeing me without curiosity, apparently not

145

at all moved by the commotion which swirled around his stall.

"Oh, Pride, you're all right!" I threw my arms around his neck — and in that instant I knew what was wrong. This wasn't Pride. This horse was black, his markings much the same as Pride's with a white blaze and one white forefoot. Still, I thought if I studied on it I'd detect some differences. This horse stood unmoving while I hugged him. Pride — the Pride I knew — would have nuzzled at my chest, especially when distraught because something unusual was happening in his stall. But this one had no curiosity in his eye and no spirit in his bearing. The whole atmosphere in the stable felt different — there was no electricity, nothing positive.

"Lonnie! This isn't Pride!" If I had been frightened when I saw Ker, I was now terrified . . . for Pride, for Ker, even for myself. What had happened to my horse? At that moment, there was no doubt in my mind that Pride was *my* horse as much as Ker's.

He was back in the stall in a flash. "Oh, now Callie, come on. You're upset about Ker and —"

"This isn't Pride," I insisted almost frantically.

"How do you know?"

I told him my intuitive feelings, and he shrugged. But he looked around the stall, finally asking, "Got a rag? A white rag?"

I shook my head. What on earth was he worrying about a rag for now? While I watched in disbelief, he pulled his flannel shirt out of his belt and pants, then tugged out the white T-shirt he wore beneath. Pulling on one end of it so that he could wrap it around his fingers, he examined the horse carefully, looking at things I could no more see than I could fly. Finally, he picked up a hind leg and began to rub with the T-shirt. In minutes, the shirt was brown — and the hind foot was white.

"You're right," Lonnie said, "this isn't Pride. Boot black, that's what it is."

"Boot black! Who . . . why . . . ?" Before I could say more, my attention went from Pride — or his substitute

— back to Ker, who still lay lifeless upon the cot. Bertelli had driven his pickup truck right next to the cot, and several of the boys were loading Ker, cot and all, into the bed of the truck.

"You ride with him, T. Joe," Bertelli ordered, and I swallowed a gasp. I didn't like T. Joe — but then I didn't think he would do anything to harm Ker. "You, too, Walter," Bertelli added, and I couldn't help thinking that Ker would be astounded at the company he was keeping, if he were conscious.

"Take him to Doctor Barnes' clinic," I managed to say, not knowing if that was what Ker would want or not. Still, Doctor Barnes was the only doctor I knew, and it seemed logical to me. My head still whirled with questions: Should I follow Ker? How would I find Pride? Where was Benjie? I literally twirled in a circle, frantic with the feeling that I had to do something. And then I sank down into the hay, at a loss to know what to do.

"Benjie?" I said, looking at Lonnie. In all the flurry, I had overlooked the obvious. Why was Ker in the stall and not Benjie. And where was Benjie, when I most needed him?

He shrugged. "Haven't seen him since yesterday afternoon. I got to go to exercises. You okay?"

I nodded. When he was gone, I sat for a while, trying to collect myself, and finally, I stood up to look this strange horse in the eye. No, it was not Pride. But it was a horse, a living animal who was not at fault for whatever had happened here. I named him "Faker" and talked to him at great length as I fed, watered, and curried. I figured morning exercises were asking a bit too much of me, even if Faker needed the workout. And I also figured if I stayed right next to this horse, sooner or later something would begin to unravel this mess. And in a bit I could use that office phone again to check on Ker.

Sure enough, Benjie appeared pretty soon, whistling so that while I was still in the stall and heard him approaching, I thought for a minute it was Ker. And then of course I realized it couldn't be, and I flew out of the stall.

"Benjie!"

"Yeah?" he replied nonchalantly, standing before me with his hands stuffed in his pockets and a slight chip on his shoulder, though I supposed it was only visible to me. "Ker around?" he asked.

"No!" I replied violently. "And why . . . where have you been?"

"Ker and I . . . we . . . uh, we agreed to disagree last night. I left his blasted horse in his care." Benjie's voice grew angry. "Where is he? I still got a score to settle."

It all came tumbling out so fast that Benjie had to say, "Whoa, Callie, whoa," a couple of times. But finally I told him what had happened, and all the nonchalance went out of him, like air leaving a balloon.

"Is Ker all right?" he asked.

With a flash of guilt, I realized that I'd maybe been more concerned about Pride than Ker. Or maybe it was that I knew there wasn't much I could do for Ker. And maybe, even more, I was afraid to find out what was wrong with Ker, what was going to happen to him. Suddenly, a picture of his parents flashed before my eyes.

"I . . . I'll call the clinic," I said, "but the most important thing is to find Pride." Then, my tone getting more demanding, "What did you and Ker fight about?"

"I didn't say we fought. I said disagreed, and I don't know it's any of your business."

"Benjie Thompson!"

He flinched, as though he really believed I was about to hit him. "Okay! I . . . I just told him I didn't think he was doing a very good job with Pride. Y'know, leavin' him too much, lettin' you do everything. I mean, migosh, Callie! The horse has a big race coming up Saturday, and Ker goes whole days without seeing about him. Yet he's the one who made such a fuss that Pride got a third run this season. It doesn't make sense to me."

Benjie sank back down into the straw after his long speech, and then added, in a mumble, "We almost fought about it."

"Fought? With your fists?" I remembered the fight

Benjie had been in the first time I ever saw him, and what a ruffian I thought him. Ker would never, I was sure, have offered to start a fight.

Benjie just nodded unhappily, confirming my opinion that the near-fight had been his idea, not Ker's. But then, Ker hadn't been himself, that was for sure.

"Ker as much as told me to mind my own business yesterday too . . . said he was the employer, and I was the employee," I said slowly.

"Yeah, that's about what he told me. So I told him he could just stay with his horse, I was going home." The cockiness erased by concern was easing itself back into Benjie's voice.

"I'm half surprised he didn't just lock the door and leave," I said, and then a bittersweet thought occurred to me. "He told me the other day he'd never leave Pride alone, only because he knew if he did I'd come spend the night . . . and he didn't want the responsibility for that."

"Give him credit, Callie. He could've left, and you'd never have known."

"It's Sloan," I said. "She's . . . well, I don't know . . . but Ker hasn't acted normal since she came along."

Benjie was studying Faker, who stood looking at us with stupid disinterest. "Callie, the most important thing is to get Pride back. He could be hurt . . . anything might happen to him. Who knows who has him and how they treat horses!"

I shook my head. "He's all right. I'm sure of that . . . well, almost positive."

"How do you know?" he asked suspiciously, and when I shrugged and admitted that I didn't know how I knew, I just knew, he raised his hands in despair.

"But I don't have any idea where to find him," I said. "I . . . I need your help." It came out as a plea.

"Go call about Ker," he said. "I'll nose around the stables."

"Can we both leave?" I nodded my head toward Faker.

Benjie almost laughed. "Sure . . . who's goin' to do anything to him? You want to lock that old barn door af-

149

ter the horse is gone . . . and this time that's the truth, about the horse being gone."

I ran all the way to the office.

The gum-chewing, magazine-reading lady was back. "You again, honey?" she asked. "Just make yourself to home. Anybody the Colonel okays is all right with me." Her look was full of inquiry, as though she were bursting to know why I was on the Colonel's good side — and why I had to make so blasted many phone calls all of a sudden. I knew that if any other stable boy had tried to use this phone, he'd have been turned away, and rudely at that.

At least, by now, I knew the clinic number by heart. I asked for Doctor Barnes and identified myself firmly as Callie Shaw when asked. It seemed to make some impression, maybe because I now was responsible for two patients at the clinic. The doctor was on the line at once. He disproved my notion about two patients at once.

"Callie, your aunt is doing fine, just fine. I couldn't be more pleased. Her, uh, attitude seems better."

"Yes," I said impatiently, "but that's not why I called. Ker Ferguson — the man who was brought in unconscious — how is he?"

"He's alive," he said, and I caught a certain dryness in his tone. "I doubt he'll want to do a lot of celebrating any time soon."

"Celebrating?"

"Yes. He . . . uh. . . I think he had drunk too much."

My mind flashed back to Ker holding his head and moaning that he'd had too much champagne. For just a second I believed the doctor, but almost as quickly I knew that was not the answer. "He hadn't been drinking too much," I said.

"He showed every sign of it," Doctor Barnes said, "and I could find no other reason for his coma. He's awake now . . . but pretty miserable. You know, headache, nausea, all the things that go with overindulgence."

150

Maybe if Pride hadn't been gone, I'd have reluctantly believed Ker had simply drunk too much. But now I knew better. Trouble was, I didn't have the time to convince Doctor Barnes by telling him the whole story.

"He'll be all right," he said. "Alcohol poisoning is serious . . . only occasionally fatal."

"I'll be there later this afternoon to see Aunt Edna and Ker both. Thank you, Doctor Barnes."

I could hear in his voice as he hung up that he was still puzzled — and slightly disapproving.

"Colonel's arrived at the track," the gum-chewer said as I emerged from the inner office. "He's lookin' for you."

I looked at the clock on her desk. Far too early for the first race. What was the Colonel doing here?

His car door stood open, the chaffeur leaning casually against the frame of the car and every once in a while bending low to say something to the Colonel or hear something that was being said. When he spied me, the chaffeur straightened into his usual haughty pose.

"There you are! About time! The Colonel came early, just to see you."

"Well, he didn't tell me that!" I said smartly.

"No need to be rude, Miss," was the haughty reply, and I fought down an urge to kick his shins. If he knew the problems that burdened me this day . . .

Before I could say a word to the Colonel, he said, "I hear Ferguson got carried away by the ambulance — too much to drink."

I sputtered. "That wasn't it . . . and how did you know?"

He cackled. "Not much goes on at this track that doesn't make its way back to me. Why do you say that wasn't it?" He seemed genuinely interested.

I told him about the switch of horses, dwelling on the fact that somebody must have sandbagged Ker so they could make that shift during the night.

The old man was silent so long, with his hands moving nervously across his robe, that I thought he didn't believe me. Then, suddenly, he barked, "Williams! Come here!"

151

The ever-ready chaffeur stuck his head in the door with a polite, "Yes, sir?" and the Colonel fired off a string of orders that went so fast I missed the details. But the gist of it was to find out what horses had been moved about — where a new horse had appeared, where one was missing, what was different in the horse scene within a radius of twenty-five miles. "And don't overlook the track stables right here," the command ended.

"Right here? Pride's not at the track," I said.

"Never can tell, girlie," the old man answered. "Stranger things have happened."

"No," I said, "he's not here." Once again, I didn't know how I knew, but I did. If Pride were that close to me, I'd have sensed it — and so would he.

"Ferguson?" the Colonel asked.

"Doctor Barnes says he's going to be all right," I told him. "I'll go see him this afternoon."

"Never did ask you," he said. "What'd you do about your father?"

I told him about my phone call, and when I'd finished, he said, "I knew you'd do it, girlie, I knew you would."

"Yeah," I said, "but now he's called the doctor, and that's the end of it. I won't hear from him again, at least for another thirteen years."

"Then that is the end of it, and now you know that," the Colonel said. "Get on with you. I want to think about this horse business."

"You will find Pride, won't you, Colonel?"

"Can't promise that," he said. "I'll use whatever I have to try, but I can't make no promises. You promise me you'll try?"

"Yes," I said, "I promise." But I didn't think there was a thing in the world I — or Benjie — could do.


Benjie's tour of the stables had netted him nothing — no information that would be helpful, not a suspicion of anything.

Not knowing anything made my fears worse. Would they kill Pride? An air bubble in a vein? At the very thought, a tremor went through me, and Benjie asked, "Now what? You getting sick?"

"No. But we have to find Pride *now*." Somewhere, I knew, the answer to all this was right before me . . . but I couldn't find it. "Benjie? Is there a horse around here you could ride?"

"A horse? Ride?" He was incredulous. "What d'ya want me to do?"

"Us," I said impatiently, "us. I'll ride Faker here . . . in fact, that's it, Benjie. Let's take Faker out on the road, give him his head, and see where he goes."

"Right back to the barn, that's where he'll go." Benjie was not enthusiastic about my plan and had not stirred from his seat on the floor. "Anyway, you got to go see Ker and your aunt."

"Later . . . I'll do that later. Come on . . . can't you find a horse?"

He grew condescendingly patient. "Callie, these are racehorses. Nobody . . . *nobody* is going to let me take his horse on a little ride around the countryside."

"Then," I said, "you'll have to walk." Without another word, I began saddling Faker.

"You can't ride him," Benjie objected. "He doesn't know you . . . you don't know how he acts . . . you'll get thrown the first minute you get on. You plain don't know enough about horses." He announced this last with a kind of triumph.

"Do you want to ride him? I'll walk."

"No." Benjie wilted before my determination. "I'll hold the bridle while you get on, and we'll see if you can stay on."

We got Faker outside, and I talked to him, though I have to confess my heart wasn't in it. I didn't talk the way I did to Pride. But still, I asked him to behave and let me ride. And he did. At least, he let me mount.

"How're we going to get out of the track grounds?"

153

Benjie asked. "Ride right through the front gate, with all the people still coming in for today's races?"

"There's a side gate," I said. "We've got to find it."

"I know where it is," Benjie said in disgust. "Come on, I'll lead." And off he trudged, heading toward the south end of the grounds.

Sure enough, a gate in the fence was held only by a hasp that was quickly undone. I rode through, Benjie followed and refastened the gate, and we were on our way. I let the reins drop on his neck.

Faker promptly stopped dead still, which made Benjie laugh.

"Don't laugh at me," I said furiously, kicking the horse just enough to get him moving and praying he wouldn't break into a canter. Then again if he did, at least we'd leave Benjie behind.

With Faker setting his own pace under no guidance from me, and Benjie following on foot, we meandered through Arlington — past stores and curious people who stared at us, past a couple of tents where people who'd lost their homes were living and empty stores that had gone bust just like Uncle Charlie. Then we were headed west, into the open country beyond the town.

We had probably gone three miles outside town — with Benjie complaining every minute of the hour or more it had taken us — when Faker started to turn into a long lane bordered by an ill-kept barbed wire fence. A sign tacked to one fencepost at the roadside said "Stables" and nothing more. In the distance were a poorly kept barn and a nondescript house.

I pulled back on the reins and looked at Benjie, who simply shrugged. "We can't ride right in there," I said, terribly aware that we were sitting out in the open. Here and there a tree dotted the landscape but it was pretty much open prairie. Anyone up at the barn or the house in the distance could have seen us clearly — though right now, I couldn't see any sign of life up there.

"Let's go," I said, kicking Faker into a canter that left Benjie behind. I rode about half a mile, then stopped to wait for him to come panting up to me. "We'll ride double into town," I said, "and then you can take Faker back to the stables. I got to see Ker right away."

"Thanks," Benjie said, still breathless. He put a foot in the stirrup I'd left empty for him and swung himself up behind me, muttering about the folly of riding double on a delicate racehorse.

"Faker isn't a racehorse," I said. "He's a fake." That tickled me enough that I began to giggle, the sound of which frightened Faker into a bolt.

Clasping his arms tight around my waist, Benjie yelled in my ear, "For Pete's sake, Callie, stop this horse."

I tried, I really did, but Faker was determined to run, and no amount of sawing on the reins was helping me. At least I did stop giggling — instantly. There was nothing else Benjie and I could do but hold on, which we did until Faker finally ran out of steam about a mile down the road. We rode the rest of the way to town in silence and didn't even say much when we both dismounted and then Benjie climbed aboard again to take the horse back to the track.

"Think anyone saw us?" I asked.

He shrugged, and his look plainly told me that he thought today I'd led him too far into my foolishness.

"I'll . . . I'll be back to the stables tonight. You be there?"

He nodded, although I didn't think he showed a great deal of enthusiasm.


Ker was sitting up in bed. In fact, he was demanding his clothes from a nurse who was muttering about Doctor Barnes and permission.

"Ker! I think we've found Pride!"

He turned his ill temper on me. "What the devil do you mean, found Pride? Where has he been?" Yelling must have hurt his head, for he winced in pain.

I couldn't believe it! Why did Ker think he was here? What did he think had happened? I backed up a little.

"How are you?"

He frowned. "I feel like six horses have ridden over me . . . twice. My head hurts, my stomach is uncertain at best, and I'd like to sleep for a week. Now what's this about Pride?

"Wait," I said, "First tell me what happened to you."

He shook his head miserably. "I don't have any idea. I just know when I lay down to sleep I began to feel really awful . . . the world was reeling and all that."

"You go out to dinner with Sloan?"

"No. She brought me a sandwich . . . after Benjie left, I didn't leave Pride. I promise, Callie, I really didn't. And Sloan, she understood . . . brought me that sandwich and a beer." He stiffened just a little. "Only one beer."

"You know how we found you this morning?" I asked.

"The way I felt was clue enough," he said ruefully, "but Doctor Barnes felt obliged to tell me the whole story. Says it could have been food poisoning — but he really thinks I drank too much. And, Callie, I didn't."

"Somebody slipped you something to put you to sleep so they could substitute another horse for Pride," I told him confidently, and then launched into the long tale about Faker and how Benjie and I had discovered that rundown stable to the east of town. "I think Pride's there, and we've got to go back out there tonight."

Ker seemed to gain strength before my very eyes. "Yeah, we do. Pride's got to run . . . and win . . . that race Saturday." He paused a minute. "You go see your aunt, while I find my pants and put them on."

I found Aunt Edna with the tennis ball clutched in her hand. "Look, Callie," she said delightedly and gave it a gentle squeeze, not enough to hold on to the ball, but a beginning.

I kissed her forehead. "Aunt Edna, that's great."

"I heard Ker Ferguson was brought in this morning. What's the matter with him?"

"Food poisoning," I said quickly. "He's okay now. I'm going back to the stable with him."

She got a look on her face that I could call nothing but silly. "He's a dear man, Callie. You keep him safe at *that* place."

If she only knew what a botched job I'd made of keeping him safe so far! After a few more minutes of visiting I left Aunt Edna, still working with her tennis ball. At least, I thought, something was going right!

Ker was waiting, fully dressed but looking a whole lot the worse for wear. "I've called a taxi," he said. Then he looked at me with just a glimmer of his old amusement, "I don't suppose you brought the truck . . . and I don't feel like walking."

I nodded in agreement and we headed out the door of the clinic. To my dismay, Ker suddenly said, "Sloan! Has anyone told her what happened?"

I could only shrug. I surely hadn't told Sloan anything, and I doubted anyone else had. Could she, I wondered, know without being told?

# Chapter 12

# A Rescue and a Reunion

I was like a runaway train, barely keeping to the track in my anxiety to get Pride back — Ker's concern for Sloan, Aunt Edna's health, even my search for my father, all fell into oblivion before the obsession that drove me.

To my everlasting horror, when the taxi dropped us at the gate to the racetrack, Ker was not as single-minded.

"I've got to eat," he said. "They didn't give me a thing at that hospital."

"Eat?" I exploded. "I thought you were nauseous." What an awful word!

"Eating," he answered patiently, "will make me feel better. Go get Benjie and meet me at the clubhouse."

The clubhouse again! There was no way I was going home to change for the clubhouse. "No. I am *not* changing clothes, and Benjie won't either."

Ker looked distinctly irritated. "I didn't say change clothes. I said meet me. Both of you." He paused a minute, then looked hard at me with eyes that lacked all that laughter I'd come to expect. "That's an order."

Grumbling, I headed toward the stables, turning

once to watch him hurry to the clubhouse. The hurry, I knew, was because of Sloan, not any need for food.

I'd already put up with nonsense from the taxi driver, who'd been talkative beyond belief, or so I thought.

"You folks work out to that there track?" he had asked, his drawl emphasizing his ungrammatical speech. "I don't know how a body can afford to go out there, things being like they are around here."

Ker had answered with better grace than he'd shown me all afternoon. "Some folks just bet once and make a winning. It's the ones that don't know how to quit that give racing a bad name."

"That's for sure," the driver had agreed. "Had a friend myself that way, feller name of Gambrell. Got hisself right in debt."

"I know Mr. Gambrell's family," Ker had said solemnly, "and I'm very upset about that tragedy."

"Just tryin' to feed his family, is all he was tryin' to do. Can't blame a feller . . ."

Ker had made small talk with the man, who drove at a snail's pace, while I sat twisting my hands in my lap and thinking I probably could have walked faster than this taxi was going.

And now Ker was putting another obstacle before me — dinner at the clubhouse. I knew I wouldn't eat a thing.

Bless Benjie! He was as angry as I was about the whole thing. "I'm not goin'," he said vehemently. "Especially not if that Sloan woman will be there. She's what Ker and I fought about in the first place, and I'm not about to eat dinner with her."

Even as I silently applauded his sentiments, I realized that we couldn't antagonize Ker at this point. My tone changed from one of indignant rebellion to pleading. "Benjie, we've got to. Ker won't go unless we do . . . and we can't get Pride back without him."

"Without him? Pride is his horse! There ought not be any possibility of Ker not going. What did he say?"

"Well, he didn't say he wouldn't go . . . he just said he had to eat, and so did we."

159

"I won't eat a bite," Benjie said, as though echoing my own thought, "and I'll be miserable because everyone will stare at us. But let's go."

We trudged toward the clubhouse — well, Benjie trudged. I danced ahead and kept trying to hurry him. Before me yawned this long, impossible time spent over dinner when we should be hurrying out to meet Pride.

To my absolute surprise — and delight — Ker sat alone at a table. "Sloan's already gone home," he said. "I called her and everything's all right, but she's tired . . . tired from worrying over me, she says. So we'll eat a proper meal and talk about what's to be done next."

I couldn't tell if Sloan's absence hurt his feelings or not. "Talk!" I said angrily. "What's to be done is we have to get Pride back!"

Ker looked pained. "Callie, could you lower your voice . . . a whole lot?" He looked across the room at the waiter who had just brought us glasses of iced tea. "Do you know that waiter?"

"No," I said, puzzled. Why did it matter if I knew the waiter or not?

"Neither do I," he said, "so we don't know if he's listening to our conversation or not."

I subsided. Benjie ordered chicken-fried steak — clubhouse or not, this was Texas — and I asked for chicken salad, something I considered a rare delicacy because I never got it at home. Aunt Edna always boiled a hen and served it with dumplings. Both Benjie and I ate every bite on our plates, after all the vows of not being able to eat. Ker, on the other hand, picked at his steak.

"Ker . . . aren't you through yet? We need to go!" I didn't mean to rush him, but I was back reeling along that track again, barely able to contain my anxiety.

"Callie," he said, holding his knife and fork in his hands like upright weapons, and leaning across the table toward me, "we cannot go anywhere until at least midnight. When we finish this meal . . . when *I* finish my meal, since you both have already wolfed your food down . . . we'll go back to the stall and sleep." As I opened my mouth in protest, he put down his fork and held his hand up, the flat palm facing me. "No, no more. That's what is going to happen."

I felt like a deflated balloon. "I won't be able to sleep," I said. "How could I, with Pride in danger?"

Hours later, Ker shook me awake, his touch gentle. "Come on, Callie. It's one-thirty. I think we can go now."

Groggily, I came to consciousness, to find Ker standing over me and Benjie already poised by the door.

"I won't be able to sleep," Benjie mimicked, adding in his own voice, "I thought we weren't gonna be able to wake you. Almost had me as worried as Ker did this morning . . . or yesterday morning."

Angrily I stood up and said, "Let's go."

In silence, the three of us walked the length of the stables toward Ker's truck. If ever the stables had been busy at night — as they had the night I'd sat on that hill and watched, and as they obviously had the night before, when Ker was drugged — they were silent and empty, almost eerily so tonight.

"There's nobody around," I said softly.

"Don't fool yourself," Ker said. "After what's happened around here, most every stall has someone sleeping in it."

I shuddered at the fear that seemed to hover over the track.

When we reached the truck, Ker astounded me by suggesting that we not start the engine. "Let's roll it to the gate," he said, nodding to Benjie, and so, with one on each side, that's exactly what they did. I steered, following Ker's whispered instructions. It might have been noisier but it sure would have been faster to start the car and drive it. I itched with impatience.

Finally, we were on the road. Benjie and I gave Ker directions to the place where Faker had tried to turn in, and almost before we knew it, we were there. In fact, we were too much there — too close for Ker's comfort. He drove right on by.

"Ker!" I screamed.

161

He turned on me, almost furious. "If you make any more noise, I will personally bash you over the head and leave you in the ditch by the road." He took a deep breath, as though to calm himself. "Now, we're going about a mile down the road, and we're gonna walk back, and then we're gonna watch for a long time to make sure that engine noise — and Callie's outburst — hasn't aroused anybody."

And that's what we did. I never said a word, not even in whispers, but I was fuming. I was sure it was three in the morning by the time we got to that gate.

Ker had unloaded flour sacks and strong leather thongs from the back of his pickup and made us carry them, though I couldn't for the life of me figure why. When we got to the barn, I understood.

At the turnoff toward the barn, Ker made us watch for a long time until he finally decided that it was all clear. Then we crept up that lane, bordered by fields now turned brown and bare, offering no shelter. Still, we crept, bent over, as though that hid us.

"Callie," Ker whispered, "you're going in that barn alone. But I want you to be very careful . . . and very quick to get to Pride before he can whinny. He'll know you, and he'll be glad to see you."

My heart beat furiously, and I wondered if all this excitement was going to give me a heart attack at an incredibly young age. "Okay," I said.

One lone light bulb shone at a corner of the barn, illuminating a circle but leaving most of the area in the dark. The house was completely dark. If there was anyone there, they were sleeping.

"Okay," Ker whispered, "go on."

I bolted on tiptoe, if one can do that, for the barn door, which had been conveniently left ajar — almost enough to let a horse through. As I went by, I gave it a shove to open it further and then shuddered as it squeaked on hinges that badly needed oiling. I wanted to call out Pride's name, but mindful of Ker's warning — and his displeasure with me — I tiptoed along a row of stalls, three on each side, all empty until I came to the last one. There, head down, was Pride.

"Pride," I called softly, "don't whinny. Don't do anything. Just wait for me." In a flash, I was inside the stall, my arms around his neck, my mouth whispering into his ear. He sensed my concern and nuzzled my chest but never made a sound.

As I turned to lead him out of the stall, I found Ker and Benjie so close behind me that I almost screamed. It was, in fact, Ker's hand over my mouth that saved us. Without a word, they bent to work — putting the flour sacks around Pride's hooves and fastening them with the leather thongs Ker had brought. Then I understood that they were doing that to muffle the horse's hoofbeats as we led him down the road.

It seemed to take five hours to reach the highway, though I was later pretty sure it must have been five minutes. When, at last, we were back on the farm-to-market road, Ker said, "Callie? Can you ride him bareback?"

With the confidence born of innocence, I said, "Sure."

Benjie put a rope halter Ker had brought on Pride and stood holding it while Ker gave me a leg up. Once I was up, Benjie handed me the rope, and Ker took the flour sacks off his hooves.

"We'll follow, but without lights," Ker said. "You just ride him home."

I nodded, whispered in Pride's ear, and we were off.

It was a wonderful night — the sky full of stars, the temperature cold, though I never noticed it, the air crisp and clear. Pride and I seemed to float down the road, and I was barely aware that his hooves ever touched the ground. Behind us, I could hear the truck puttering along, but it seemed distant. I had the wonderful feeling that Pride and I were alone in the darkened Texas countryside, riding as though in a dream.

Too soon for me, we were at the racetrack. Once again,

Ker parked the car a distance away, outside the gate this time, and we led Pride quietly to his stall.

"Faker!" I said suddenly. "We can't put him in there with Faker."

Ker groaned. "How dumb can we be? We should have ridden Faker back to that barn."

Benjie had the answer immediately. "We'll put Faker in Golly Gee's stall. I'll look after him. And Callie, you best ride Pride in exercises. Show everyone he's in fine shape."

Ker looked thoughtful. "Wait a minute," he said. "That's just what we don't want to do. We don't want everyone to know Pride's back . . . at least not the people who took him. Benjie, put Pride in Golly Gee's stall . . . but stay with him *every minute*."

Benjie nodded, while I started to argue. "I'll go with Pride —"

"No!" Ker said quickly. "You'll ride this other horse Faker in exercises."

"I will not!"

"Callie," he said patiently, "please trust me on this. Whoever took Pride will know he's gone, of course, but we don't have to hang a red flag in their faces. Maybe . . . I don't know. This just seems much better to me."

By four o'clock we had Pride settled in Golly Gee's stall, with Benjie asleep next to him. I slept soundly on the cot in Pride's stall, next to Faker. Ker, refusing to go home and leave me alone, slept in the hay next to me. And I never knew a thing until way past daylight when Ker shook me awake.

"C'mon. Time for exercises." He went in search of coffee, while I tried to comb my hair and splashed water on my face, in a vain effort to look awake.

I was half asleep when I mounted Faker and rode out to the track, but my mind cleared suddenly when I saw Bertelli and Chance waiting at the rail. For just an instant, the expression on Chance's face was beyond belief — startled, confused, absolutely uncertain what to do next. And I knew in that second that Chance knew I was riding Faker, not Pride. He just hadn't expected us to carry out such a bluff.

Faker was definitely not Pride. It was like riding the horse that pulled the milk truck, after flying around the track on Pride. Faker was fast enough for respectability — he'd shown that when he bolted with Benjie and me both on his back — but nowhere near fast as Pride. His gait was uneven, and he lacked the spirit that Pride had. I never said a word in his ear as we circled the track.

Chance had recovered his composure by the time I pulled Faker up next to him, but Bertelli looked ashen.

"Morning, Chance," I said cheerfully. "You think he's ready for tomorrow?"

Chance looked at me, and I gave him credit for control. "No," he said shortly. "I don't think he's ready. He's been run out too much, and he'll lose. You won't find me riding that bangtail tomorrow." He turned on his heel and left.

It was a complication I hadn't foreseen. Chance would, of course, refuse to ride a horse that he knew was a substitute — a poor substitute. And besides, how could we produce Pride at the last minute and say, "Here, Chance, ride this horse. I know you won't let him win."

Benjie didn't think for one minute it was a problem. "You'll ride Pride," he said with a certainty that scared the daylights out of me.

"Me?" I squeaked. "I'm not a jockey. I can't —"

"No rule says you have to be a jockey," Benjie said.

Ker was more thoughtful. "I don't know. If you were to be injured, Callie, I'd never forgive myself. But you do know the horse."

I looked from one to the other and back again, unable to believe what I was hearing. But as I looked at the two of them, their faces dead serious and yet somehow hopeful, my fright — no, it was panic — at the thought of riding in a race turned to excitement.

"Do you really think I can do it?" I asked, my voice rising in anticipation, though I never did quite squeak that time.

They nodded.

"I . . . all right, I'll try." I felt as though I had just committed myself to riding the length of Texas.

"We've got a little more than twenty-four hours," Benjie said. "Not much time to teach you everything we know about racing." His tone was more than a little pompous.

"I will ride Pride as he wants to be ridden," I said slowly, careful to pronounce each word deliberately and clearly. That stuff about holding until the last, saving his strength, edging out other horses and jockeys was not for me. "Pride will either win it because he's the fastest or he'll lose it."

Benjie threw his hands up in the air in disgust, but Ker looked at me long and hard and said, "Okay by me." Then Benjie was really disgusted.

And it got worse for poor Benjie when Ker ordered him to stay with Faker. "Callie, you curry Pride, talk to him, do whatever you do to pump him up. But then by midafternoon, I want you out of here. I'll drive you to the hospital, you visit your aunt, and then you go home and get a good night's sleep. I'll pick you up in the morning."

"I'll walk," I said defiantly, needing to keep my ordinary routine so that I somehow hung onto myself in all this dizziness.

The day flew by. I took care of Pride and spent a long time asking him about the race. I sensed that he wanted to run, and that he'd leave the gate fast and keep the lead.

"Doesn't he need some exercise today?" I asked Ker. "He's getting stiff just standing here."

"Probably true," Ker said, "but I haven't the faintest idea what to do about it. I do *not* want him seen around this track until post time tomorrow."

Even though Pride was right in front of us as we talked, I turned around and explained it all to him. Oh, I still didn't really believe in magic, but somehow the bond

166

between me and Pride was forged because I talked directly to him. It had little to do with the words — they mattered only to me.

Ker disappeared at post time — to see Sloan, I knew — but he was back sooner than I expected, with no explanation or apology. Good-hearted, happy Ker was keeping his own counsel. But he wasn't laughing as much and he sure hadn't been whistling the last two days. I was pretty good at figuring out what was in Pride's mind, but Ker was beyond me.

"Sloan coming down here later?" I asked.

"No," he said shortly. "She doesn't know Pride's here. I told you . . . *no one* is going to know."

"How about Lonnie and the other stable boys?"

"Far as they know, this stall is still empty — we're just using it for sleeping space."

And carrying pails of water into it? Ker was fooling himself, I thought, but he was probably right to make as little fuss as possible.

Ker brought his silks, which had been cleaned from the last time Chance had worn them, and I tried them on. To my chagrin and embarrassment, they were a little tight. But they'd do for one race.

Before I knew it, Ker was herding me toward his pickup, announcing it was time for me to see Aunt Edna.

"Ker," I asked as we drove along, "can't I come back and sleep in the stall with Pride?"

"No," he shook his head determinedly. "A good night's sleep in your own bed — that's what you need, especially after last night. I expect you to win that race."

He pulled up in front of the clinic, and I opened the door to get out. Then, on impulse, I leaned over to kiss his cheek. "Thank you," I said, and was gone, hearing him sputter behind me.

Doctor Barnes was at the front desk, and I stopped to ask about Aunt Edna.

"She's fine . . . just fine," he said, a shade too heartily. I began to wonder if she was really all right, the way he was talking. "Doctor?"

167

"Run along now, Callie, and go see your aunt."

Puzzled, I walked down the corridor and turned into her room.

A man stood by the edge of the bed, someone I'd never seen before but whom I knew instantly. He was not tall — probably my height — and he was square and stockily built, with a slight paunch around his middle. He wore corduroy pants with a soft shirt of some kind and a rumpled jacket. But his eyes were blue, clear blue, and his hair had once been red, though it was now peppered with gray.

"Callie?"

Aunt Edna said not a word but just watched us.

"Callie? I'm your father." He made no move to hug me or move toward me, just stood there and let the news dangle.

"I figured," I said. "When . . . how did you get here?"

"Train. Left right after I talked to the doctor."

I looked at Aunt Edna, willing her to say something, but she remained an interested spectator.

"Why?" I asked.

"I been stubborn too long," he said. "Edna's attack," he nodded his head toward her, "made me wake up and smell the roses, as they say."

As far as I was concerned, it was something a lot less pleasant than roses that he smelled.

"It was good of you to come," I said mechanically. Way back in my mind was the conviction that he had not come to meet his daughter — and might never have come for that reason. He'd come out of guilt, because the sister he'd quarreled with had nearly died.

"Let me look at you," he said, moving toward me until he could put his hands on my shoulders. He held me at arm's length, but it was only my face he inspected. "You look like your mother."

"Aunt Edna always said that." My chin rose. "But she says I have some Shaw about me too."

He smiled, almost ruefully. "That you do."

168

I turned to Aunt Edna to inquire about her well-being. She was noncommittal, saying she felt fine.

"Doctor said she could go home tonight if someone would watch her," my father said. "I told them I would, but she says she'll wait until Sunday, when you can take care of her."

"Did you get the horse?" Aunt Edna asked.

I nodded, and would have said no more, but she goaded me, saying, "I've told your father about that horse you take care of, but he has a different opinion than I do."

I was willing to bet that my father didn't believe in the devil. "He's a good horse," I said, thinking what an untold story lay behind those words.

Aunt Edna was nobody's dummy. "There's a lot going on I don't understand, Callie, but you've no need to tell me. I've just sensed it when you've been in here. But one reason I'm staying here is so that you and your father can get acquainted. You tell him all about that horse . . . and about Ker Ferguson."

I opened my mouth to protest, but she added, "And feed the man some supper. He's hungry after eating Fred Harvey meals on the train for a day and a half."

"Yes, ma'am," I said obediently, leaning to kiss her on the forehead. Aunt Edna could pretend to be brusque about this, but I knew she was making a big sacrifice in a couple of ways — staying in the hospital, and not launching into one of her tirades about the evils of racing.

"Come on," I said to my father and marched out of the hospital room.

We walked in silence. I truly didn't know what to say to him, and he seemed not inclined to talk, though I caught him now and again casting a sideways look at me. Mostly, though, he walked with his eyes a little down, as though watching the ground.

The way home from the hospital led by a butcher's shop, and as we passed, he asked, "Need something for dinner?"

I debated. There was, I knew, little at home, maybe

the makings of cornbread or a few potatoes. "Some sausage might be nice," I said.

He bought sausage, just enough for two, and I boiled it with potatoes. Nothing in the icebox was cold, for with Aunt Edna gone and me barely home, no one had let the ice man in. Everything in the box was warm, spoiled, and threatening to go to mold. I cleaned it with baking soda, and my father said he'd get a new block of ice in the morning.

"Pretty bare larder," he commented. "You and Edna makin' out all right?"

"Good as anybody these days. There's a Depression . . . or isn't there one in California?"

He grinned self-consciously. "Yeah. We get all the people who leave Texas," he said, and I remembered Jimmy Don Russell. "But I'm one of the lucky ones," he said, "not much affected by it."

"Aunt Edna says we're lucky too," I said. "We got a roof and we eat regular meals. 'Course now she can't take in ironing . . ."

"Take in ironing!" he exploded. "My sister is taking in other people's ironing?"

"What did you expect her to do?" I asked, unable to hide the bitter tone in my voice. "Train horses?"

"She'd be good at it, never doubt that, young lady," he said. Then he put his head in his hands, as though it hurt him, and sat silent for a long time. I had no words to comfort him. He was the one who'd stayed away and never written or called. I wasn't about to share his guilt.

"What should I call you?" I finally asked him, and he raised his head.

"How about Bobby? Everyone else calls me that, and I'm not sure I'd be used to 'Father.'"

"Okay . . . Bobby."

Just as quickly as it came, his unhappiness over Aunt Edna and the ironing disappeared. "Tell me about this horse." He straddled a kitchen chair backwards and watched me as I sponged out the inside of the box.

170

"Poco's Sweet Pride . . . he runs in the final race tomorrow."

"Who's the jockey?"

"I am."

He exploded, strings of unconnected phrases coming out of him, about danger to girls, no girl should ever ride in a race, what was Ker thinking of, he was going to find that Ker idiot — he actually used that word! — right then and tell him what was what.

"You through?" I asked, tightening my grip on the door of the icebox. When he nodded, I said, "Good, because I am riding tomorrow, and there's nothing you can do about it."

He subsided, his anger gone as quickly as it had come, which amazed me. I wasn't used to people who went so quickly from one mood to the next. But when I saw that he was calm, I asked, "Do you want to hear the whole story?"

He nodded, and I told him. Where Aunt Edna would have been gasping with horror at Golly Gee's death or Pride's kidnapping, my father just nodded. To him, it was an unfortunately familiar tale. When I told about stealing Pride back during the night, he rubbed his hands with glee and said, "That's my girl!"

"You really think you can win?" he asked.

"No," I said, "but Pride can win. All I have to do is be there to satisfy the requirements. Pride could win without a jockey."

He looked skeptical but shrugged. "I'll be there," he said. "I want to meet Ker . . . and see what happens."

I shrugged. I didn't know how it made me feel to think that my father would be watching me ride. All I knew was that finding him was not what I'd dreamed. I'd expected Prince Charming, who had an unbreakable story to tell which would explain his silence. Instead, I had a slightly overweight, slightly shy man who said nothing about why I hadn't heard from him in thirteen years.

"Okay," I said. "I'm leaving early in the morning."

171

"I'll go see your aunt and be at the track by noon," he said.

We went to bed shortly after that, with carefully formal wishes to each other for the night and a sound sleep. It wasn't exactly like having a father to tuck you in.

# Chapter 13

# And the Winner Is . . .

Next morning I slept till a scandalous nine o'clock, waking to the smell of coffee. Bobby was in the kitchen, more cheerful than I'd yet seen him, singing "Scotland, The Brave" which made my heart turn over. His hands were in a bowl of flour.

"How d'you like your eggs?" he asked. "I'll have these biscuits in the oven in just a minute. Got to get you off on a good start today."

"Haven't got time," I said, "I'm hours late. Why didn't you wake me?"

"Sit down," he said. "Ker's been here, brought coffee, these eggs, and said to let you sleep as late as you want. Nobody was going to ride that horse in morning exercises anyhow. Now, how d'you like your eggs?"

"Scrambled," I said uncertainly, taking the cup of coffee he handed me and dosing it liberally with sugar. It was nice to be rescued from Aunt Edna's pale tea. "You don't have to fix my breakfast."

"I know that," he said, showing no signs of stopping.

Cooking was the last talent I'd expected him to have,

and I watched, my mouth probably hanging open in surprise.

"Did you . . . you never did . . . ?" My question hung in the air.

"Marry again?" He looked at me shrewdly. "No, whatever else you may believe about me — and a lot of it is probably true — I loved your mother. Never did find anyone to take her place . . . and didn't look very hard."

Intuition told me that he and I were this moment, over coffee and eggs, closer than we were ever likely to be. It was the time to ask him why, but I didn't think I could bear the answers this morning. With no more talk, I ate my eggs and biscuits — he made a fine, light biscuit — and then jumped up saying, "I really got to go."

"Ker's coming back for you at ten."

I needed that long walk alone to sort out my thoughts, to focus on the race and forget about Bobby Shaw and Aunt Edna and all. "Tell him I went on," I said. "He can drive you to the clinic."

And that's apparently what happened, for I was at the stables a good hour before Ker arrived. For the first time in days, he whistled as he walked along the row of stalls, and he kept whistling as he came through the door of the stall where Pride and I waited.

"Ker! I thought you were only going to sneak in here so no one would know about Pride."

"No secrets on a racetrack," he said cheerfully. "I got a feeling everybody knows. But, Callie, I also got a good feeling about this race."

"Good," I said a trifle bitterly, for my eggs and biscuits were sloshing around in my stomach, propelled by butterflies of anxiety. But I wouldn't tell Ker that.

"That father of yours," Ker said, "he's a fine fellow. I had a good talk with him this morning."

"Good," I managed, thinking that maybe Ker wasn't the judge of people I'd thought him. First Sloan, then my father. Not that I disliked Bobby — I just wasn't sure I was ready to call him "a fine fellow."

"He's proud of you . . . why, when I told him how you

tricked your way into this job, and how quickly you picked up racing knowledge, and how Pride took to you, he just about burst his buttons. Said you were a true Shaw, through and through."

"My family's raised horses for generations," I said. "That part of what I told you wasn't a lie."

"I know, Callie, I know. But give your father a chance, will you? He's . . . he's almost afraid of you."

Afraid of me? How could a grown man who'd ignored me for thirteen years be afraid of me? "Hogwash," I said and considered telling Ker to mind his own business.

He sensed my mood and tactfully changed the subject. "Callie, be sure to tuck your hair up tight as you can. Some folks will know who you are, but I'd rather not tell the whole world a girl is riding my horse."

"Why not?" I demanded, angry now that he would hide the fact that I was a girl. Poor Ker, he couldn't do it right this morning, no matter how he tried.

"'Cause they just wouldn't understand," he said peaceably, "and you're not going to start an argument with me about it. Benjie will go with you when you weigh in, and you let him do most of the talking."

"Who's posted as the jockey?" I asked.

"C. Shaw," he told me. "You think I was going to write out Calpurnia?"

I was still on the edge of anger. Ker looked at me and said, "Callie, don't be looking for things to get angry about. I know you're nervous . . . but you got to get over that and stay calm. Pride can tell."

I took a deep breath, knowing Ker was right.


I refused lunch and Ker didn't push it, though he brought me a hot mug of chicken bouillon from the clubhouse. I sipped it gratefully, feeling its rich warmth spread through me and enjoying the hot afterbite — it had, he told me, red pepper and was therefore supposed to energize jockeys.

175

Maybe it was Ker's bouillon, or maybe Benjie's obvious nervousness when we went to the weighing room, or maybe it was when I saw the crowd in the grandstand, I lost concern for myself and began to think about Pride. Whatever it was, all my anxiety drained away as I walked toward the saddling area, having successfully weighed in at less than the legal weight.

When Benjie led Pride up to me, I wrapped my arms around his neck and told him it would be all right. He nuzzled my neck, pushing at me, and I thought there never was a more wonderful horse. Most of the jockeys and some of the stable boys eyed me curiously. They had no idea who C. Shaw was. Big dumb Walter frowned at me, but Lonnie brushed by close enough to say, "Watch yourself!" with a grin on his face.

Chance was there, preparing to ride for Bertelli, a horse named Faraway Thunder, owned by none other than Robert Burke. He glowered at me but said nothing.

As we paraded toward the starting gates, I saw Ker and my father leaning against the railing. Bobby gave a thumbs-up sign, and I returned it. A little way down the fence Bertelli stood, looking glum. When I rode by, he lowered his eyes.

At the gates, Pride stood calmly, though I could feel energy coursing through him. I patted his neck, whispered in his ear, and told him to run his own race.

Chance, however, was having difficulty with his horse. It spooked and balked at the gate, once rearing back so that Chance almost lost his seat, and then refused to enter the gate again. Watching carefully, it came to me that the problem was not the horse but Chance. Cleverly, he was goading the horse, an old delaying tactic Benjie had told me about — get the other horses good and nervous waiting at the starting gate. Though it seemed to me it would also make Faraway Thunder more nervous than Chance had in mind.

At last, we were away. Pride flew out of the gate at a respectable pace but not with the great rush I had anticipated. Three horses, none familiar to me, were in front of us. Though Pride ran steadily and strongly, he showed no inclination to catch up with them. We rounded the first turn into the backstretch, and suddenly Pride let go with a tremendous surge of energy.

The wind whipped at me — and blew my cap off. I could feel my hair losing its pins and streaming out behind me, like some sort of a banner. An extra roar went up from the crowd, and I knew they had discovered that a girl was riding in the race. But beyond that, it all seemed unreal.

I rode as though I were floating . . . other horses, fences and grass, even the cheering crowds flew past me with a fuzzy quality, as though they were dreams and the only real things in the world were Pride, me, and the track. We thundered along the backstretch and were almost to the turn when, out of the corner of my eye, I caught a horse gaining on us and doing it in a sideways fashion. It was Chance on Faraway Thunder, and he meant to bump into Pride. He was deliberately aiming for us.

For just the flicker of a second, I let panic set in. If that horse bumped Pride, he'd lose his stride at best. At the worst, I'd get dumped on the track, just in front of the pack of horses behind us, so that their hooves could grind me into sawdust. But that thought lasted only as long as it takes to blink an eyelid. Just as quickly, I leaned over Pride's neck and whispered in his ear, "Trouble to the left . . . let's get out of here, Pride!"

And the horse that I thought had been running as fast as he could let loose with another burst of speed. As we pulled away from Chance, I cast one backward glance at him and saw only murderous eyes, so cold and angry they frightened me. Then we rounded the turn, flew down the homestretch, and I forgot everything but the triumph of victory. Faraway Thunder, the closest competitor, was four lengths behind us.

I heard the roar as we crossed the line — and yet I didn't. I was so focused on Pride, so fearing that he'd burst his heart (I'd heard of that happening) that I almost didn't enjoy our great moment of triumph. Pride's speed was so great that he was still running as we rounded the track to the backstretch, though I was leaning into his head, willing him to slow down. Gradually, his speed lessened, and we walked around the turn into the homestretch, where a jubilant Ker, a smiling Bobby, and an absolutely out of control Benjie were waiting.

We had won! Pride was the champion, and Ker was a rich man. Well, not rich . . . but the purse would pay the bills for his racing season, and justify another year at the track, no matter what his family said.

I slid off Pride's back and went immediately to hug him. We stood, both panting, my hair hanging in wet ringlets down my back, through the presentation ceremonies. Ker accepted the prize money graciously and acknowledged his jockey — that was me! — with gracious words, but never said anything about my being a girl. I blessed him silently.

When Benjie came up to take Pride for his cool-down walk, I said, "No, I'll walk him." And so we walked once more around the track, me talking all the while about how wonderful he was and Pride's panting slowly subsiding until he was breathing normally. I could feel the crowd's eyes on me all the while. I have never been more conscious of being a girl. But as I walked, section by section, those people stood and cheered. I almost cried from happiness.

Sometime during that mile-long walk, I remember Chance and his murderous eyes and I wondered what lay behind that look. It was more than a jockey's anger at not being on a winning horse, more even than anger that a girl was beating him. Trying to puzzle out Chance, I was only vaguely aware that way off in the distance, I heard a pop or crack. It was a sharp noise I couldn't identify.

As I led Pride off the track and back toward the stables, I pulled him over to where the Colonel's car was parked. The chauffeur looked astounded to see me leading the day's big-winning horse as though I had some old mule behind me on a halter.

178

"I want to introduce Pride to the Colonel," I said.

Even that nasty old chauffeur could grin, though he tried to hide it as he bent into the car. In a minute, the Colonel stuck his head around the edge of the car frame. I guess getting out of the seat was too difficult for him.

"You won, girlie . . . and I knew you were the jockey." He laughed in pure delight. "Knew you were a winner."

I pulled Pride's nose down until it touched the Colonel's outstretched hand and then saw a smile of happiness on his wrinkled face. "Fine horse," he said. "Fine horse."

"My father's here," I told him. "Arrived yesterday."

"And?"

"It's okay," I said.

"Good." He called the chauffeur over and muttered something in his ear. The chauffeur's grin was slightly less now, but he fished in his own pocket and handed me seven dollars.

"No sir, I can't take that. I haven't solved anything," I said. "Pride's safe and won the race, but we don't know any more than we did about who killed Golly Gee or who doped Pride or why." I'd been so carried away with the race that I'd truly forgotten all that for a minute.

"Keep it," the Colonel said. "I bet you'll find out yet."

As I tried to hand the money back, and he stubbornly refused, neither of us had any idea how soon his words would come true. Finally, I thanked him and headed for the stables.

"See you next year," I said, and he chuckled.

"I 'spect I'll see you 'fore that. You can always get a message to me through the horse farm."

"Yes, sir," I said, and gave the chauffeur a kind of farewell nod, which he returned about as half-heartedly.

"Come on, Pride, Ker will be having fits."

Actually, I thought, he wouldn't. He'd be in the clubhouse, celebrating with Sloan. And that's probably where he was, for I didn't see him when I first rounded the corner to the stables. But from that moment on, I forgot about him too.

The stable boys all milled around in a knot. Benjie, seeing me, broke loose to come say, "Don't go down there, Callie."

"I got to put Pride up and curry him," I said.

"Not now," Benjie said firmly. "There's been an accident."

Ker? My father? Who? "An accident?" I echoed.

"Looks like Bertelli shot himself . . . Lonnie found him, and the police are down there. But . . . well, just take Pride back around the corner until they take the body away."

Now I was aware of horses whinnying in nervousness and of a hushed babble of voices, voices which couldn't stand to be quiet and yet which were kept soft out of respect — or horror — of the occasion. I had hated Bertelli, or tried to, sure that he was behind Golly Gee's death and Pride's doping and all the bad at the track and knowing that he disapproved of me. And yet, I couldn't forget his concern and his instant action when Ker was in trouble. Probably, I was rational enough to think that he was like the rest of us — some good, some bad — and his death made me sad.

Benjie took Pride's reins and led both of us aside, Pride making a soft noise behind me.

"See? He'll get nervous too. Take him off a ways. I'll go get a blanket and a currycomb."

"No need," Bobby said, walking up behind Benjie with those very things in his hands. "Knew you'd need these. Callie, you couldn't get to your stall if you wanted . . . police have it blocked off."

"Why would Bertelli shoot himself? Just because his horse lost the race?" That didn't make any sense to me at all.

Bobby shook his head. "There's more to it than that, my girl, a lot more. But I'll be darned if I know what."

Before he could say more, Ker and Sloan appeared on the run. Apparently the news had reached the clubhouse. It was Sloan who led the way, taking great rapid strides, while Ker did a limping half-job in a futile attempt to keep up with her.

"Sloan!" he called.

When she whirled on him, her eyes reminded me of Chance — they were filled with the same kind of hate. Ker stood looking blankly at her, and I thought he might melt like a piece of ice left in the sun. Sloan resumed her run, barging through the group of stable boys like a tornado, running past the policeman who tried to stop her.

"What's gotten into her?" Benjie asked, but Ker only shook his head. He looked grim though, as if he'd just found out his best friend was his enemy. And maybe he had.

It was late afternoon — almost suppertime, my stomach told me — before we got Pride settled back in his stall. The police had departed, presumably taking Bertelli's body with them, and the crowd had cleared. We'd seen no more of Sloan, and a subdued Ker had stayed by his horse's side all afternoon.

Bobby stayed with us, too, and at one point Lonnie stuck his head in the stall. "Heard you were here, Shaw," he said, and Bobby turned with surprise.

"Lonnie!" His voice was cautious as he said, "How're you doing?"

"Well enough," Lonnie said. "Was stabling for Bertelli, him that killed himself."

Bobby just nodded, waiting.

"It's over, Shaw," Lonnie said. "It was a long time ago, and I don't want to fight that battle anymore. Besides, your daughter's all right." He gave me a tight smile. "Callie, see you next year?"

"I hope so, Lonnie, I really hope so."

After he left I looked at Bobby. He shrugged and said, "Horse business breeds a lot of bad feelings. Lonnie and I were on opposite sides once . . . and my side won. I still say I was right, but so does he. He was a jockey . . . and now he's barred from riding."

Bobby's face was like a map of his emotions. Clearly

181

he was unhappy about what had happened and yet still felt all right about what he'd done.

"I never cheated a man or a horse," he said, "and that's the truth." Then he added ruefully, "But I wasn't always that smart about them who were cheating me."

I reached out and took his hand. Whatever had happened between him and Lonnie was one of those things that might never be puzzled out.

I asked Ker about Sloan, and he just said, "She's gone. I . . . I've known for three days she would be."

Ker insisted we have dinner in the clubhouse — "one last farewell meal," he said. He made every effort to be the cordial host, offering a toast to the best girl jockey he'd ever seen and winking at me, challenging Bobby to move to Texas to train race horses, even offering Benjie a job for the year. Benjie politely declined, since he planned to go back to the Three-D Horse Farm. I had the sense of being surrounded by people I cared about — and even wishing Aunt Edna were there — but the thrill of victory I'd felt earlier in the day was gone.

Now triumph was bittersweet, marred by the puzzle of Mr. Bertelli and Sloan and Golly Gee and my failure to do what I'd promised the Colonel.

I never did solve any mysteries that summer. Somehow, they solved themselves. Bertelli had left a long letter among his papers detailing how he'd done whatever he had to do to rig the races. What startled all of us was that he'd done it under the direction of Robert Burke, a man desperate to own Arlington Downs.

"It was more than money," Ker told me later. "Burke wanted it to be his racetrack, not the Colonel's, and he figured the way to do that was make it so dangerous to race here — dangerous to the horses — that the Colonel would give up."

"And Bertelli?" I asked.

"Burke was blackmailing him. He even killed Golly

182

Gee himself just to show Bertelli what he could do. Remember? It was after that Bertelli really started to act scared."

"And Sloan?"

"She's Bertelli's daughter and Burke's girlfriend."

I gasped, and he looked rueful. "I figured out right quick that someone like that wasn't going to fall head over heels for a Texas ranch boy with a limp and a paunch. I sort of played her own game on her. She was supposed to be getting information from me, and I figured she was easier to watch if I stayed by her side. But all the time she thought she was helping Burke, she didn't know he was blackmailing her father. Poor Sloan."

Ever the romantic, I whispered, "But I thought you were in love!"

"So did I," he laughed, "for about ten minutes." Ker's quick laugh didn't hide the pain that flashed across his eyes, and I knew Sloan had hurt him. I pitied her because of her father — since I had just found my father, sort of. But I hated her for what she'd done to Ker.

Chance had been part of it too, working for Burke, throwing races and even doping horses with that elephant juice he'd talked about too much. That was why he acted so funny the time Pride ran like mush. Chance had been the one who doped him. He knew all about the kidnapping, maybe was even part of it.

When Burke found out Pride would run, he ordered Chance to see that Pride didn't win — no matter the cost. Burke had to be in control, and Chance went along with him for the worst of reasons — money. When it all came to light, he was barred from racing. I wondered if he'd become a stable boy like Lonnie, but somehow I couldn't feature that. Chance disappeared, and we never heard any more about him.

Robert Burke was told never to come to Arlington Downs again, though the Colonel would have had to enforce that by his own private means. Nothing was ever proven against Burke, and he lost only his good reputation. I never knew what happened to Sloan. She and

Burke deserved each other, but I couldn't imagine even Sloan staying with the man who'd caused her father's suicide. Good riddance, wherever she is, I thought.

Colonel Waggoner kept Arlington Downs, of course. There never was much doubt about that. Robert Burke trying to outsmart the Colonel was like a mosquito attacking an elephant.

Bobby went back to California, with promises to return for the season at Arlington Downs the next year. Ker drove us into Fort Worth, where Bobby caught the train, and it would have been a silent ride, if the two of them hadn't talked about horses and racing. I listened, and sometimes I looked at Bobby, and then back at Ker, and I felt like I had two fathers — two very different fathers.

"You take care of her," Bobby said to Ker, and I felt invisible. But then he gave me a hug, and I thought his eyes looked a little funny when he said, "I'm glad you found me, Callie. I guess I always wanted to be found."

As the train pulled away, I stood shading my eyes against the sun and straining to see him. He waved once, and then was gone. And I was back where I started, with no father. Well, not quite.

Ker put his arm around my shoulders and began to whistle softly, "Oh ye take the high road," as we walked back to his truck.

When Aunt Edna came home from the hospital, Ker announced that he needed a housekeeper and would Aunt Edna . . . could she . . . ? The work wouldn't be strenuous . . . It turned out that Ker did most of the work himself to spare her, and Aunt Edna ran his house according to her will. She hadn't been happier in years.

And me? Ker and the Colonel settled my fate between them.

184

One November afternoon, five long days since the end of the season, Benjie was sent as their messenger. I was listlessly cleaning house and wondering what was next in my life when Benjie arrived, breathless, at our door.

"Callie! Callie!"

"Calm down, Benjie," I said crossly. "You'll wake the devil that walks amongst us."

He was too high on happiness to pay any attention. "There are no devils anymore. Only good fairies." And then he laughed uproariously, while I stood, broom in hand, wondering whether or not to swat him with it.

"Benjie Thompson, what on earth is the matter with you?"

"A horse," he said, "Kincheloe put me in charge of one of the yearlings. It's mine to train."

Even though jealousy was a strong part of what I felt right that moment, I really was happy for him and tried to let him know.

"There's one bad part," he said, but the look on his face was anything but sad.

"What could be bad?" I asked.

"Got to hire you as stable boy," he said, laughter spilling out as though this were the best joke ever.

"Me?" I asked weakly. "A stable boy at the Colonel's farm?"

"He insisted," Benjie said. "Kincheloe told me so."

Ker's pickup sputtered along right about then. He parked, got out, and stood looking at us a minute, shaking his head. Then, as he walked, he said to me, "I told this young fool I'd drive him over here, but he couldn't wait two seconds until I finished my business. Had to run all the way."

Benjie just stood grinning.

"He tell you?" Ker asked.

"About working for the Colonel?" I nodded yes and the broom fell unnoticed to the ground.

"That's only half of it, Callie," Ker said. "Colonel and I have come to an agreement about this and — well, you can be a stable boy, but you've got to finish school. Got to make up that two years you lack."

Benjie looked uncomfortable. "I was gettin' around to that," he said slowly. "It's part of the deal."

"Who said?" I asked belligerently. "And whose deal?"

"Mine," Ker said firmly, "and the Colonel's. Take it or leave it."

"School started two months ago," I said, sure that would solve the matter. You couldn't just waltz into the classroom any old time during the year, and next year I'd face the same problem — racing season came during the school term.

"You can start now and catch up," Ker said. "I checked with the school district."

"I'm too old to go back to school . . . all my friends are gone . . ." My voice trailed off as I sought more excuses.

"They tell me you can probably make up the work in a year." Ker remained firm.

While I considered this, Ker delivered his final blow.

"Pride's goin' to be boarded at the farm. Benjie may need some help."

"Pride?"

He looked at the ground, a bit unhappily. "Yeah. You and Benjie can take care of Pride . . . and I'll be up ever so often to check on him . . . *and you.* But I'm goin' back to help my folks on the ranch. Till next season, that is."

Ker Ferguson, I thought, you're too good to be real. I hoped his mother would love him and his father would respect him all that he deserved.

And that's how I came to be a stable boy. They still call me that — at the Three-D Farm in Arlington. Benjie and I take care of Pride and Sunny Boy, the chestnut he's training, and we still fight near as much as we talk. But the other day, when I got ready to leave, Benjie punched me lightly in the arm, and when I turned around indignantly, he planted the lightest of kisses on my nose. It almost made my stomach turn over.

# About the Author

JUDY ALTER is the author of historical novels about women in the American West, including *Cherokee Rose* (loosely based on the life of Oklahoma cowgirl Lucille Mulhall); *Jessie* (directly based on the life of Jessie Benton Frémont, wife of explorer/soldier/statesman John Charles Frémont); and *Libbie* (reconstructing the life of Elizabeth Bacon Custer, wife of General George Armstrong Custer). Her earlier novel, *Mattie,* won a Spur Award from Western Writers of America as best western novel of 1987. *Luke and the Van Zandt County War* was named best juvenile novel of 1984 by the Texas Institute of Letters, and her short story "Fool Girl" won a Western Heritage (Wrangler) Award from the National Cowboy Hall of Fame.

Alter's books for young readers include *Maggie and a Horse Named Devildust, Maggie and the Search for Devildust, Maggie and Devildust — Ridin' High!, After Pa Was Shot,* and *Katie and the Recluse* (all published by Ellen Temple of Lufkin, Texas and distributed by Eakin Press). She has also written several nonfiction "first books" for children: *Growing Up in the Old West, Women of the Old West, Eli Whitney,* and *The Comanches* (all published by Franklin Watts, Inc.).

Alter has been director of Texas Christian University Press since 1987. She holds a Ph.D. in English with a special interest in the literature of the American West from TCU, an M.Ed. in English from Northeast Missouri

State University, and a B.A. from the University of Chicago. She is a past president of Western Writers of America and secretary-treasurer of the Texas Institute of Letters. In 1989, she was named one of the Outstanding Women of Fort Worth by the Mayor's Commission on the Status of Women.

The author is the single parent of four now-grown children. A native of Chicago, she has lived in Texas for thirty years.

---

OTHER BOOKS BY JUDY ALTER

Maggie and a Horse Named Devildust
Maggie and the Search for Devildust
Maggie and Devildust Ridin' High
After Pa Was Shot
Katie and the Recluse

---

(Published by Ellen Temple, Lufkin, Texas and distributed by Eakin Press)